JUICY BITS:

Erotic Stories of BDSM, Kink and Fetish

Edited by Angel Ackerman and Ralph Greco, Jr.

AUTHORS:

Aravielle

Angel Ackerman

Dani Brown

M.Christian

W. S. E'das

Ralph Greco, Jr.

Liam Herne

Olivia

William D. Prystauk

Angie Ravenstone

J.Z. Sharpe

Juicy Bits: Erotic Stories of BDSM, Kink and Fetish
Copyright 2023 Parisian Phoenix Publishing/Angel Ackerman
ISBN 978-1-957863-18-4 Paperback
Published by Parisian Phoenix Publishing, Easton, Pennsylvania USA

Cover Illustration: Joe Swarctz, josephswarctz@gmail.com

PHOTOGRAPHERS —
Angel Ackerman
Eva Parry
William D. Prystauk
Joan Zachary

ILLUSTRATORS
Andrea Bruno
Joe Swarctz

C O N N E C T with the publisher:
Substack: parisianphoenixpublishing.substack.com
Web: www.ParisianPhoenix.com
Facebook   @parisianphoenixpublishing
Instagram: @ parisianphoenix
LinkedIn   @parisianphoenixpublishing
Patreon   @parisianphoenix
TikTok   @parisianphoenix
Twitter: @parisbirdbooks

C O N N E C T with the editors:
email Ralph: ralphiedawriter@gmail.com
email Angel: angel@parisianphoenix.com

Contents

Explore Sex With Your Clothes On

Written language has magical powers. Hear me out — whether you are a reader, a writer or someone just looking for something to spark your imagination or your libido, you have to admit that words stir so much in us. We use them to hurt one another, help one another. We use them to educate, to persuade. And even to arouse. The origins of this book, like much of modern life, finds its roots in an eclectic hodge-podge of accidents.

But I can tell you that its contents and arrangement are very intentional. Representation matters. And while there is no shortage of erotic material to consume, and there is no shortage of BDSM stories to share, this book aims to explore various fantasies, kinks and fetishes AND show them in a way that highlights consent, negotiation and safety.

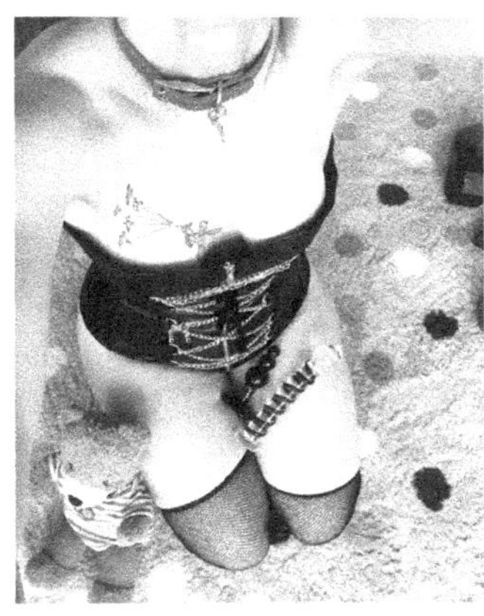

To that end, we have also arranged this book, as my co-editor Ralph Greco Jr. puts it, from "mild to wild." That way, if a story feels like it's too much for you, you can put the book down. We also labeled the beginning of each story with a sexual content list, so you're not surprised. We want your knowing consent before you turn each page. A lot of material featuring BDSM, kink or fetishes doesn't fully explain consent or safety measures or phrases like "RACK" (risk aware consensual kink) and "safe, sane and consensual." So we tried to demonstrate some of those negotiations here.

We start the book with debut authors Olivia and her story, "First Date," where the main character is introduced to the idea of BDSM and move to Aravielle's "A Day at the Beach," which uses nudity as an impetus for self-reflection and vulnerability in a group setting. But by the end of the book, we hope we've given you a safe place to explore chastity, impact play, fisting, breast play, work fantasies, smoking fetishes and even some delicious sadism (in a *menage-a-trois* setting). The writing styles vary as widely as the sexual topics. Because you never know what might turn you on. I remember lying on my mother's bed, sneaking peeks at the copy of Anais Nin's *Little Birds* that she hid in her underwear drawer. I was too young to fully understand erotic stories, and perplexed by some of these strange encounters in the book, but too fascinated to stop reading. I want to recreate that feeling.

The book includes published erotica authors Ralph Greco Jr., M.Christian and Dani Brown. There are a couple names, mine and that of William D. Prystauk, who have published before but not in this genre.

Come into the book with an open mind, and if you don't like what's happening in a story, skip to the next one. Another phrase often mentioned in the kink world is "don't yuck my yum," a reminder that no two people respond the same way to anything. Some of the scenes in this book may seem normal to you, obscene or even overwhelming to someone else. You may encounter things you never imagined or things you've always wanted to try. Whether the book makes you curious or confirms your place in the vanilla world, this book is a safe place.

We encourage you, our readers, to use these stories to start conversations especially with your bedroom partners. Because communication remains the key. Everyone deserves to be heard. Everyone deserves affection and touch. We need to be honest about our desires, our likes and dislikes, and encourage more con-versation about consent and sexuality that does not perpetuate feelings of guilt and shame.

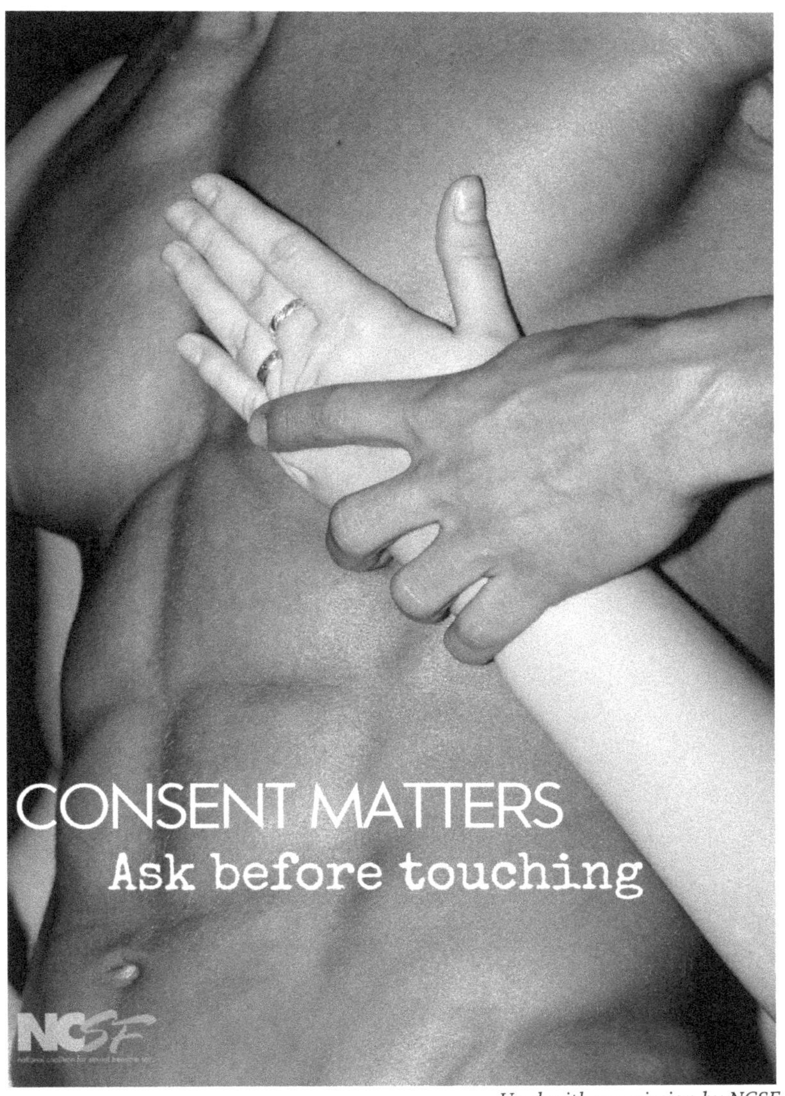

Used with permission by NCSF

Goals

By Angie Ravenstone

(In no particular order)

- make you laugh

- let you cry

- help you sleep

- love you

- fuck your brains out

- feed you beer and chocolate

First Date

By Olivia

"I think you need someone to take care of you," he said.

I laughed. "Noooo, I'm pretty sure I can take care of myself. I've been doing it a long time now. In fact, it's usually me taking care of other people."

I expected him to smile, but he looked at me quite seriously, his blue eyes skeptical. Just as I was beginning to feel uncomfortable under his gaze, he said, "Of course. You care about people and you show that you care by serving them."

He paused, but before I could protest the term 'serving them,' he added, "serving in one way or another." And he smiled.

His smile was warm and touched his eyes as well as his lips. It was just a bit... It was a bad boy smile, I thought. Just a touch. Or... not bad boy exactly. No, it was the smile of someone who knew things.

It kindled something in me and I wanted to make him smile more.

By the time I had sorted that out in my mind, I had been quiet too long, and for a second, I couldn't remember what I was going to say anyhow. He was watching me, perfectly comfortable with my silence.

"Well, I can't imagine what kind of 'taking care of' someone would offer me," I said. "I mean, I don't need somebody protecting me, or telling me the right thing to do."

Just a hint of a smile on his face now. I waited, curious, head tilted just a bit to one side. He paused long enough that I was

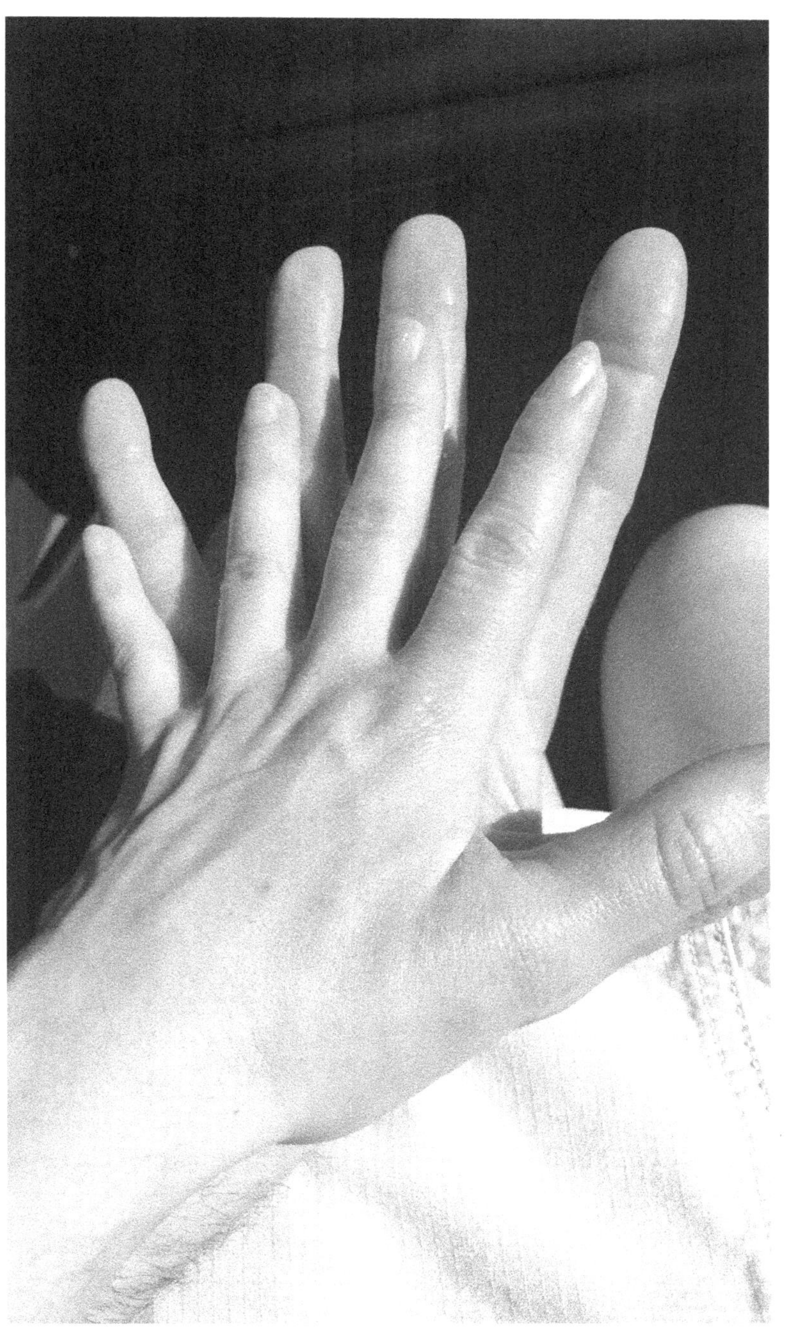

getting uncomfortable. Then he laid his left hand on the table between us, palm up.

"Let me see your hand, please," he said.

Slowly, I brought my hand up, and would have laid it in his so our palms were touching. He stopped me, turning it so my left hand laid palm up in his hand. He had not touched me before.

It was, after all, a first date. Dinner had been delicious and we had talked about our lives. Relaxed and comfortable, he had drawn me out and I'd shared more than I usually would on a first date.

But now, with my hand nestled in his, I felt my nipples getting hard. I squirmed in my chair and noticed some heat between my thighs. Damn, I told myself, I know it's been a while but he is just holding your hand. Stop it.

"I don't know you very well," he said, his eyes on our hands. "But I think that when you, anyone, carry other people's burdens a lot of the time, you also need time to stop and let it all go. Do you ever feel that way? That you'd like to be able to relax and let go, just for a while?"

"Sometimes," I said softly.

It felt strange to admit this, but it was so true. Sometimes I had fantasies about someone telling me what to do. I tried not to think about those fantasies, but they were really vivid in my mind right at that moment. Looking at his hands, I could imagine them touching me, guiding me, and a little shiver ran through me.

He smiled, just for a second, and I wondered if he had noticed. I would have pulled my hand away, but he looked at me and shook his head.

"Don't," he said, adding, "please."

I had already obeyed though, before the 'please,' and he knew it.

"Good girl," he said, and smiled again.

His words lingered in the air. Good girl.

I bit my lower lip, embarrassed at the rush of pleasure those words gave me. I couldn't look at him, I knew he was watching me, but I didn't want him to see my reaction.

We sat in silence while I carefully avoided eye contact and tried to think of something, anything, to say to break the silence. Frozen, I couldn't think of a thing. My hand was still on top of his hand on the table, palm exposed, and I wanted to pull it away, but didn't want to… I didn't even know what I didn't want to do. I just knew that I couldn't move.

He leaned forward and laid his other hand on top of mine. Now my hand was sandwiched between both of his, warm and comfortable and soothing. I felt protected somehow. I still didn't look at him, I focused on our hands instead.

"Your hand is so small," he said.

I nodded. I felt small, my hand disappearing between his. His hand was large, the fingers more slender than I would expect, but long. Gently, he squeezed my hand, massaged it a little bit, and I smiled.

"You are a good girl, aren't you, Alina?"

His words echoed in my mind. A bit unreal, I mean, I'm not a girl and maybe not so good, but in that moment, I could only think, 'yes, yes I am.' And I wanted to be, I wanted him to think I was a good girl, to be pleased with me.

"Look at me," he said.

Slowly, I raised my eyes, nervous and unsure of myself. His eyes were smiling, his lips just turned up a bit.

"I want to ask you some questions, please. Will you answer some questions for me?"

His voice was gentle.

I couldn't look away, I nodded and bit my lower lip again.

"Say 'yes' if you agree to answer my questions," he prompted me. "Can you do that?"

I could feel my heart pounding, I could barely breathe. I felt like a rabbit, trapped by his hands, by his voice. I wanted to answer his questions, and I was afraid of what he might ask me. But he was waiting for my answer, I had to speak, even though my mouth was so dry I could barely form the words.

"Yes," I said, hesitant, tentative. "I will."

He grinned then, and I felt my heart melt.

His attention was so powerful, so seductive. I was happy to answer his questions.

"Alina," he said, "Have you ever been in a relationship where your partner expected you to please him by doing what he asked of you or what he told you to do?"

I shook my head, no.

"Use your words," he said, which made me laugh.

"No," I said, "No, not really."

"Not really?"

"No, I mean, of course, your partner always kind of expects you to please him and do what he asks. But half the time, you can't figure out what they want, and I'm not sure they even know what they want either."

He nodded, quite serious. "So they weren't clear about what they wanted, and of course you couldn't just figure it out. Is that right?"

"Yes, that's it exactly. I mean, maybe I would have done what they wanted if I knew what it was!"

"Yes!" he said. "I think… No, let me ask you. Are you someone who likes to please the people in your life, who likes to give from your heart?"

I felt so uncomfortable, I didn't know what to say. I mean, yes, I did like to please people, but that was stupid and weak, and maybe I was too giving, and I didn't want him to think I was stupid and weak or easy. But I couldn't lie, I couldn't say no. Tears welled up in my eyes, and I couldn't speak at all.

"It's okay, little one," he said.

His voice was so gentle that my tears spilled over. With my free hand, I started to brush them away, but he stopped me. He caught both of my hands in one of his, and with the other hand, he gently traced the tears on my cheek.

So many feelings rushing through me. I felt that he had captured me, was containing me, my hands still held firmly in his hand. And that felt good, secure and comforting, I didn't want him to let me go. At the same time, my heart was pounding and I could barely breathe. I had no idea where he was taking me, I was terrified and thrilled.

"Tell me," he said, his voice deep and silky. "I will ask again. Are you someone who very much wants to please, do you open your heart and give generously of your love and of yourself?"

"I… Yes, I do want to please and… and I try to give… to give my love," my voice trembled. "I don't think I'm very good at it though."

More tears fell, and he held my chin and stroked my cheek with his thumb. I leaned into his hand, welcoming his touch.

"I think maybe you have not been with anyone who could teach you how to please them, or who would appreciate all that you have to give," he said. "Even now, you are pleasing me with your openness and giving me parts of yourself that I don't think you share with everyone."

I felt a warmth that started at my core and spread through my whole body. Now, I definitely wanted to please him. I think he could have asked me anything in that moment and I would have happily done it. I sighed, content.

But he wasn't finished.

"Has anybody ever spanked you? Maybe just for fun, or maybe when you were a naughty girl?"

The heat between my thighs was fast and fierce. I squirmed in my seat. This was my guilty secret, the one I had never told anyone. I longed to be spanked. For fun or for punishment, it didn't matter. It seemed like I had always wanted to. But I had never, ever told anyone.

And he didn't ask me if I wanted it... just if anyone had! I could say no, and he would never guess. I started to say at, to say no, but...

"Or maybe no one has done it, maybe you've just thought about it. A little fantasy here or there."

He was watching me closely. I was blushing, I knew I was. I might have well had "spank me" tattooed across my forehead.

He grinned. "Maybe I should ask if you touch yourself when you think about it. If you slip a hand between your thighs, stroking your hot wetness..."

He was waiting for my answer. I wanted to answer, but I was so shocked and embarrassed and... Well, turned on. I was really hot. All those feelings just froze me.

He laughed.

"Alina. Look at me."

Slowly, I raised my eyes to his, and in that moment, all my concerns slipped away. My focus was totally on him.

"One step at a time," he said. "Have you ever had a fantasy about being spanked by someone?"

I was still embarrassed, but it wasn't so hard to answer now.

"Yes, I have."

He nodded approvingly. I felt a little rush of relief, and a flare of heat between my legs.

"When you have those fantasies, do you like it? Does it arouse you?"

His tone was so cool and clinical, like he was just collecting data. It almost made it easy for me to say yes even though I was still uncomfortable.

He nodded, matter-of-factly.

"When you are aroused, do you touch yourself?"

"Yes."

"Are you able to have an orgasm?"

"Yesssss," I said, blushing, my nipples hard as pebbles.

Again, he just nodded. I wouldn't have been surprised if he'd gotten out a clipboard and started checking off boxes on a form.

He smiled and I took a deeper breath.

"Enough."

"Did I pass?" I asked, almost laughing.

He chuckled.

"You did very well," he said. "Let's try something else. I'm going to ask you a few more questions, but this time, when you answer me, I want you to say, 'Yes, Sir,' or 'No, Sir.' Do you understand?"

I paused, I had not called anyone 'Sir' before, not since I was a child. But I was curious about what it would feel like so I said, "Yes, Sir! Yes, Sir, I understand."

"Good girl," he said, favoring me with another smile.

A rush of pleasure ran through me. I had not ever felt that before, not just suddenly like that. I wondered if he could tell.

"Have you heard of BDSM?"

"I… Yes, of course I have. I mean, *50 Shades of Gray* and all that, right?"

"Is that a new way of saying, 'Yes, Sir'?"

His tone was light, teasing.

I quickly said, "Oh, sorry. Yes, Sir! I have heard of BDSM."

"Much better, Alina," he said.

The server approached our table, coffee pot in hand. He shook his head and gestured for the check. I was more disappointed than I would have expected. I thought there would be more questions. This seemed so anticlimactic. And it was still early, not even 9 p.m. yet.

We were silent until the server had left the check.

"Did you know there's a BDSM club near here?"

"No… Sir," I said, barely remembering to add the honorific.

"There is," he said, glancing at his watch," And I'm supposed to be teaching a class there in about an hour or so. I had thought I'd be taking you home first, but now I'm wondering if you have any interest in attending class with me. No strings attached, no one would touch you or pressure you to do anything you didn't want to do. But I'm teaching BDSM 101 and I have a feeling that this might be important information for you to have. Would you like to come with me?"

Without hesitation, I said, "Oh, yes, Sir. I would like that."

We left the restaurant together. He reached for my hand, but encircled my wrist with his hand instead. I felt his gentle restraint with a secret thrill. I smiled and followed his lead like a good girl.

A Day at the Beach

By Aravielle

Another beach day and it was everything I needed. Once I made it there. The traffic was terrible. Lots of accidents. Reckless people everywhere... ruining other people's good time. I went for the harder, feel good, sometimes angry music.

Nickelback. Saving Abel.

All of this keeps me calmer about reckless people. Cool it down now.

More Nickelback. Blacktop Mojo. Lynyrd Skynyrd. Disturbed. Foghat.

Finally at the beach. My nude beach. An hour later than planned but you can't be late to the beach... It waits for everyone and anyone.

I happened upon William who is cute and kinda sexy. He is very chill, confident and he likes naked beach bling. Not too much though and I think it's adorable. Do what makes you feel good. We have been beach buddies once before and left with a hope we see each other again. He's good company. Today I told him I remembered his name because he taught me something (where the term 'redneck' originated) in our last happenstance.

I had been listening to Chris Stapleton when we started talking. He stuck. I am terrible with names. I also told William I owed him a drink that first day.

William is a kindred spirit for sure. I've told him as much. We covered so much ground before I thought to ask what he did for a living. He's a therapist. Go figure! I told him I've had a therapist for

almost 30 years and didn't realize I needed another one. I told him he could send me a bill if he wants. I now owe him five or six drinks.

It's very easy to talk to him, and now I realize why. He has found his calling. One of the things we talked about was "getting your shit together." He mimicked back to me what I wonder so often:

I'm afraid if I truly get my shit together, then I'll be bored.

I share with him my verbal image of a Gothic Tinkerbell and he has an interesting theory. He says, "I feel like your Gothic Tinkerbell is a true part of you."

It's becoming more clear to me every day. Gothic Tinkerbell will be my tattoo. My one and only tattoo. William asks where I would have it done. I don't know yet. I feel like I will know where she belongs when I am meant to know. She is a work in progress. I never got a tattoo because I could never commit to something.

When I get a tattoo, it must be something very, very unique. What is more unique than a tiny part of your own soul drawn on your skin? Note to self: find an artist, a damned good one.

I ask William what his story is. He knows a lot about me and I know little about him. He says his girlfriend tells him to go and enjoy the nude beach by himself. She doesn't enjoy it as much as him and she understands he needs that alone time.

He says, "I can hang out and have fun, but I'm not dating anyone here."

There are boundaries.

"So, can I buy you that drink or the 10 that I must owe you now?" I ask.

He says that would be okay. He is a lucky guy and she is a lucky girl. They treat each other with respect. I would not tread on that even if I wanted to.

William did tell me that he has been in relationships where he goes headlong into it, knowing full well that it will be a complete disaster — but it will be a damned good story and memory.

Boy, I feel that. Careless, not reckless.

William asks me If I am more of an observer or do I like to be watched. I say neither, truly, because I don't usually notice much beyond my direct periphery on the beach.

"I think you like to be observed, mostly," I tell him.

He nods his agreement.

We admire good boobs on the beach and what we each thought made them so good. Today is a great boob observation day.

"I just passed a woman and she had the greatest boobs I think I've ever seen," I say.

The boobs were full and a little droopy like mommy boobs. The girl on the beach to one side of us, the one with short blonde hair, has young, full, perky boobs.

As if on cue, someone walked by.

"Now those," I say, "are kind of strange boobs."

"Well," William says, "there is a penis attached to them."

I nod slowly. I had not seen anything below the belly button. So, that explained it.

I tell William I feel sadness for the women who feel like they have to have those big, fake tits.

William keeps checking the time. Small chit chat follows. I apologize for my mind dump on him. He says he enjoyed it. When he leaves, I get up and dip in the water to cool off.

I walk past a group of women that I had not noticed prior. One of them points at me.

She yells out, "Great boobies!"

I laugh and smile at her.

"That's my line," I admit. "I just usually don't say it out loud. Right back at you."

I float in the water for a while, and when I come back onto the sand I notice the group I had interacted with is six, very attractive women. They are all very touchy and kissy.

I imagine I could have been in the mood for that another day, but I am not today.

I absolutely need chill and quiet today.

There is a couple very close to me. She is young, chill and confident. Good for her. It has taken me a long time to get there in life. And sometimes still, I am not always super chill or confident.

He is a little bit restless. It seems like he is there more to keep her company.

My battery dies on my phone and I debate leaving, even though I'm not quite ready. Yes, this is a theme with me. I'll forget my charger or grab the wrong cord. It's a whole sensory experience for me to go to the beach. When my music is taken out of that equation, it changes the whole dynamic.

Without my music, I start to get in my head and think too much. That is exactly the opposite of what I'm trying to achieve. I also start to notice the sweat, the sun becomes a little too hot or I feel sand where it's not most comfortable and the flies! Suddenly, I obsess over the flies. Then, I key in on the multiple different kinds of music playing around me. It all becomes sensory overload.

I start to feel restless. Maybe I'll go fly a kite in the bay. William and I had touched on that. Neither of us had flown a kite in so long, we couldn't remember.

"Why not?" I asked.

"I just never think of it," he answered.

At the time, I nodded because I understood that. That is what I am trying to reconnect with: the things that make us feel great, but are easily forgotten.

I watch the most attractive couple walk past me. It is hard to define what exactly attractive means to me. The woman has what I consider the perfect feminine body with no dimples or flaws. Her skin is a creamy pink. She has fabulous curves on her. Her hair is a beautiful shade of lighter red and it's natural. I color my hair a dark fiery red, dubbed chocolate cherry. I would guess she was close to 30.

After I noticed how beautiful she was, I turn to the guy. They are holding hands. He has an attractive body and what look like, from the distance, tattoos. They seem to be really happy with each other and themselves. I think that is what was the most attractive part.

I have seen all that I could hope for, experienced all I could today on the beach. It was a fulfilling day with a lot of beauty, lots of good feelings. I pack up my things and walk toward the parking lot to do my normal. I clean myself up as well as I can at the outdoor showers before I go back to the car. Then, I usually change in the parking lot, lotion my tanned hide and try to look like a 'citizen.'

While I do all of this, I let the car cool off. This is my routine.

Fred coined the term 'citizen' for me, a long time ago. 'Citizen' means seeming like you can fit into normal society. It's a charade. No one is truly a citizen.

I am annoyed at the type of people I encounter in the parking lot. Bad driving, loud, trash everywhere in the way of everyone. This place is all about 'leave no trace' That gets right up under my skin. Sometimes I want to scream, "If you can't respect it, get the hell away from it."

But who the hell am I?

I turn to my music for sanity. I play Jackson Dean. His voice soothes me.

Halfway through the second song, I realize what I am listening to and it makes my heart twinge, badly. I feel a little heady and sick. There are dogs and families and children. This is not where I belong. I am trespassing. I need to leave that all alone. Just let it rest. Get a kite and fly it anywhere else. I grab my fueled drink (coconut milk, pineapple and apple juice) and leave.

I am missing someone.

The music as I run from my emotions: Blacktop Mojo, Godsmack, Jackson Dean.

Even the boobies at the nude beach can't ease the fact that it is the wrong time, the wrong place and you belong where you are and that isn't with me.

But the sun and the ocean breeze on my skin, my music and the boobies are a decent consolation prize. For now.

What would William think of that?

Kim Gets Everything She Asks For... and More

By Ralph Greco, Jr.

"I don't think Kenny ever need know about this, do you?"

"I think Kenny would very much love knowing about this, don't you?" I teased. "If we were doing something...which we are not."

"You know what I mean."

"Kim..."

I kinda, maybe, kinda did, if I allowed myself to maybe, kinda, entertain what the little blonde was getting at, and see her point. But as my cousin's wife and I had never EVER been close, in 'that way,' and as Kim had been Kenny's wife now for the past thirteen years, I hadn't logged her into my 'girls I want to rub up against,' spank-band. I was more than slightly surprised that even with us sharing her bed this blustering wintry night that even a tickle of a thought of naughtiness had run across her brain, enough to make her think not to tell Kenny about us laying side by side.

Firstly, it was she who had suggested we get in her and Kenny's big bed to ride out the storm. Secondly, even though she knew my sexual fluidity had led me far and wide, I didn't ever — EVER — hit on a woman I knew had no care for, nor had ever had even a hint of a design, for another woman.

And third and most importantly, this was my cousin's wife!

"Look, we both know how bad you are."

"I'm not bad, I'm just drawn that way," I said in my best Jessica Rabbit drawl, still not turning to the woman.

"'Free spirit' maybe, that better?"

"Okay."

"And I know you are assuming,…"

Jesus these hetero housewives who think reading *Fifty Shades* gives them some insight beyond their staid suburban sexuality. I lifted up, and spun to confront my cousin's bob-haired wife's assumptions, and whatever kind of tease she was ramping herself up for at my expense.

"Um, you called because you didn't want to be alone. Kenny called because he didn't want you be alone. I came over because I agree, nobody should be alone in this weather, and we could have a few drinks and diss my cousin for having taken the kids, this weekend of all weekends, to my aunt's in Florida. So, damn him, okay?"

"But, if I remember correctly, it was you who said, 'We should just both sleep in the big bed tonight,' right?"

"Yeah," she said looking down. I guessed that pout from under her bangs worked on Kenny, or at least had to have at one time in their lives.

Sure, Kim was cute and sure, she knew it, but really what was this all about? Was she trolling to light a spark she and Kenny she didn't have anymore? Did she figure she'd grab the opportunity for a walk on the wild side? Did she want to simply see if she could get me worked up enough that I tried something just so she could find some sort of ego affirmation rebuking me?

"So, good night," I said, reached over, kissed Kim's creamy white right cheek, her left pressed into her hand resting on her pillow, then turned my back to her again.

"Man, give a girl a complex, why dont'cha," she giggle-pleaded, just as I turned my back to her fully again.

Jesus, where were we going with this? I could get my pinpoint nips hard and my hairless puss puss wet for just about any intrigue (especially intrigue), but I really just wanted to get some sleep. We had drunk more wine than I expected, and I knew we'd have lots of shoveling to get to in the morning.

'Freaking Kenny, nice time to leave bro,' I scolded my cuz silently.

Flipping over again, I spat: "Turn over and go to sleep."

"Janine."

"Turn…" I said, sat up, and pushed my cousin's wife face down.

"SMAT." I landed a quick pat on her long silk shorts. "…enough already. Go to sleep."

"Oh fuck," Kim groaned as I spied the unmistakable movement of the little blonde executing a quick downward piston with her hips.

"Jeez, come on," I thought to myself, but staying where I was sitting up over Kim, her little ass too close not to smack again, I simply reached down, and with one swoop, pulled the back of her loose shorts down over her high two-small-scoops-of-a-rump, revealing a high-cut, sky-blue pair of tight panties perfectly showing off her backside bump-page and the creamy white side orbs of her booty.

"Now that's a sight," I said as Kim clearly undulated into the bed and I gave her ten high smacks, all dead center of her hard ass. By the third she was popping up to meet my hand, by the eighth I was feeling a definite wet tickle, but by the tenth, I was pulling up her shorts.

"Now, stop this shit," I said, flumping back down on the bed and turning my own ass to her.

"Kim," I heard Janine moan. "Kim."

Yes, I knew what me spanking her like that could elicit. But I was hoping that the shock of what I had done, and the fact that I gave her a quick thrill would bring her round to her hetero-honed sense, and leave me the fuck alone. I really didn't want to get into this with her.

Really.

Really.

Couldn't she just lie there quietly and masturbate over the ass swats she obviously had loved but been totally surprised about? I could get myself off just by a few wiggles and quickly recalling the mind's-eye picture I now had of Kim's panty-clad pert buns. If I turned to her, if we really progressed further, I had no idea where this could lead, and I wasn't in the mood to set Kim and me into a cliché. But, man, her ass did look good, as it always had, granted I had just saw more of it up close and personal then I usually did. This 40-year-old-house-wife and mom of two had managed to keep her petite little body as well tended and showroom ready as she did her and my cousin's Tudor here on their cul de sac. And God knew, I could probably do exactly what I wanted with her, as Kim would be letting me lead as probably let loose with "Oh, oh no, Janine, we can't do that" pleading all along the way.

Maybe if I just kept it to…

"You're not gonna let me sleep, are you?" I said, and fell out of bed.

Before Kim had time to roll over or even really consider what I was doing — not that I even had a clear idea what I was doing — I stepped around the bottom of the bed and then up to her side of it.

"Stay exactly where you are," I said, standing over with my thin lips pursed.

I wasn't pissed, but I had to have her think I was, or, at the very least, in complete control. Which, I kind of, was. As Kim looked over her shoulder at me, I gave the command I knew would make or break the moment...and something that even with my experience in seducing seemingly shy girls out to try something they never would have admitted they wanted, was not my usual go-to.

But I knew it would work perfectly with my cousin, and me, right then.

"Take them down, all the way, panties, too."

Kim sighed, then reached behind herself and with one pull released her shorts and panties up and down over her ass. Wiggling and pulling she got her ass completely bare.

"Now," I said.

"SMAT, SMAT."

I connected my big right palm once to each cheek. "You come from this, fine. You don't, fine. But this is all we are gonna do, 'cause you deserve it."

"Nothing else, got it?" I growled and not waiting for an answer I began to smack her ass, cheek to cheek, pinning Kim to the bed as much from the force of my smacks as the fact that she unabashedly pushed her crotch into the bed and ground her pelvis through the thirty high and hard hits I gave her. Okay, I didn't exactly count, but somewhere in the one section of my mind that wasn't focused on the tight hard cheeks blushing under me (and trying to get a peek between Kim's legs, even though trapped as they were close together with her undies hammocked at her upper thighs) I knew I had landed about thirty smacks down on that great ass and she had come at least two times roiling her hips into her big four-poster, burying her face in her pillow as she did. I was pretty damn wet by the time I stopped, softly managed to step away from the bed and said:

"Pull...pull them up."

Somehow, I managed to walk back around the bed and lay down even though I had really wanted, and knew I probably could have damn well managed, to strip down my sweats and lay my aching bald pussy against Kim's hot blushed ass, grinding myself to an orgasm and her to maybe another.

"Goodnight," I said to her the big bay window revealing the heavy falling snow through its slatted curtain.

I heard Kim move, and it damn well felt that she has slid off her side of the bed. I didn't dare even look over my shoulder or turn. Another coy gaze from under those bangs, seeing maybe as much a blush across her high-cheekbones as well as the one I had just left on her ass, would have been my undoing, a close second to how making her bare ass red had nearly made me lose my senses. I had as much got her off as taught her a lesson and let her walk on the wild side for a couple of minutes, and now my cousin's wife and I had a secret, whether I liked it or not.

And I wasn't so sure I did.

So, whatever she was doing, I hoped she was simply steeling herself to now go to sleep.

"Like I said," Kim managed, after clearing her throat. "We both know how bad you are."

"Yeah, I guess," I said, wiggling into a nice side sleeping position.

Thankfully the heat in my crotch was abating ever so slightly.

"I think you need this as well as me."

I could hear her still moving around, fumbling for a second for God knows what, then she was back leaning across the big bed, placing her hand on lower back. Then Kim was pulling my sweats down and completely off my legs!

As I lay back in shock, as much as desire, I saw Kenny's little wife standing over me with the belt she had obviously pulled from her jeans hanging off the low chair to the side of her bed, where she had thrown the pants when we had undressed to get ready for bed (me in her bathroom, her in her room).

"My turn," she said and lifted the belt, as I turned to lay fully on my stomach.

Now, wouldn't my cousin Kenny like to see this, I thought.

The Supplicant

By Olivia

She waited anxiously, trying to slow her breathing.

They probably won't take me anyway, she thought. Who knows how many candidates they've had?

She took a deeper breath.

But they did call me in for an interview.

She felt her heart pounding.

She was alone in the room, a small anteroom with a desk and a chair, a floor lamp, and the straight-backed cane chair she was sitting in. She could smell the flowers, white and purple lilies, arranged in a vase on the desk.

There was an intercom on the desk too. When she'd entered the room, she'd heard it "click" and then a male voice had spoken. In a pleasantly deep voice, he'd directed her to sit, adding that she would be given further instructions in a few minutes.

She squirmed in her chair, which seemed to get more uncomfortable every minute. She wanted to scroll through her phone, but part of the invitation to interview had included making some commitments ahead of time. She had agreed not to use her phone, or any technology, during the several hours that she would be here. She had worked hard to make it to this point of the process, and wouldn't jeopardize her chances because she was uncomfortable and wanted to distract herself.

She was pretty sure they wanted her to be uncomfortable. He wanted her to be uncomfortable.

That thought made her squirm in a different way. She was acutely aware of her arousal, the heat between her thighs, her nipples slightly hardened. She started to cross her legs, then remembered that they had asked her not to do that either. Subtly, she thought. It wasn't a *Story of O* scenario. No one had told her she needed to keep her legs open. No, they'd asked her to wait "in a posture of mindfulness."

And of course that meant both feet on the floor.

A click from the intercom got her complete attention.

"We're ready for you now," the voice said. "You may leave your bag or purse under the chair. You may stand up now, and remove your panties. Place them in your bag or purse and then knock on the door across from you."

She was already standing when he got to the part about her panties, and she froze. Really? She had to take them off NOW?

But you already knew, she chided herself, that you'd have to get naked. This is just panties, you still have everything else on.

Her skirt was relatively long, hitting her mid-calf. She glanced around the room. Was there a camera somewhere? Maybe, but she didn't see it. Carefully, trying not to expose herself more than necessary, she slipped her panties off, letting her skirt cover her again as quickly as possible. She tucked the panties into her purse, turned back toward the door, and...

Paused. She paused with her hand raised to knock.

Fuck, fuck, fuck, this is insane, am I really going to do this?

The intercom clicked. The male voice returned with a hint of laughter.

"To knock or not to knock, that is the question. Whether 'tis wiser..."

Before he could finish, she knocked on the door, firmly, three times, as directed. The voice laughed.

The door opened. It was dim in the room, she couldn't see more than a few feet beyond the door. A woman blocked her entrance, smiling.

"Welcome, Naomi," she said. "Congratulations on making it this far. Put this on, please."

She handed Naomi a blindfold.

Naomi took the blindfold, feeling a bit befuddled. Her eyes were adjusting to the dim lights and she thought she could see a man, no, maybe two or three men, seated in a semi-circle further in the room. She did not want to wear the blindfold.

The woman who had answered the door, who introduced herself as Sonya, quickly guided her in putting on the blindfold. It was some kind of stretchy material and fit quite tightly, snugly. Naomi was in complete darkness now. Sonya took her arm and pulled her a few steps farther in the room, and Naomi heard the door close behind her.

"The candidates are not allowed to wear clothes in here," Sonya said. "So, I'm going to take them off for you. Do you agree to this?"

Naomi's mouth was suddenly so dry. She didn't think she could talk. She knew that if she didn't agree to this, she'd be eliminated from the competition. She licked her lips.

"Y... ye... yes, I agree," she stammered.

"Ma'am," said Sonya. "You may call me 'Ma'am.' Try this: 'Yes, Ma'am, please take my clothes off.'"

Naomi wanted desperately to tear off the blindfold and run. But she also wanted desperately to do this thing she had started, to be the winning candidate and be allowed to stay.

So her voice was low and shaky, but she said, "Yes, Ma'am, please take my clothes off."

"Good girl," said Sonya.

Naomi's top was a loose knit and Sonya slid it off over her head easily. Naomi was wearing a lacy bra and Sonya tugged it down so the nipples were exposed. They were already half-hard, but Sonya rubbed and tweaked them until they were fully extended. Then, she unhooked the bra from the back, and removed it completely.

"There you go," said Sonya, "We'll make sure they stay nice and hard now."

Naomi blushed with embarrassment. Only the skirt was left. It took Sonya only a moment to tug it down, leaving it pooled around Naomi's ankles.

Naomi moved her arms as if to cover herself.

Sonya laughed. "No. Hands behind your neck, please."

Slowly, reluctantly, Naomi raised her arms, clasped her hands behind her neck.

Once her hands were in place, Sonya said, "Elbows back please. Check your posture."

And something inside Naomi fell into place. Blindfolded, naked, exposing herself to people she didn't know, accepting dominance from some strange woman, she felt something loosen inside herself.

"Yes, Ma'am," she said.

She pulled her elbows back, which thrust her breasts out. She shifted her body to open her legs a bit, not too much, just shoulder width apart. She felt Sonya's hand slip between her thighs, stroking and caressing her swollen outer lips. Naomi shivered with pleasure, a slight smile on her lips. All she had to do now was obey.

THEMES: familiarity/neighborhood incest, forbidden encounter, impact play, pushing boundaries, spanking

Visiting With Cousin Kim

By Ralph Greco Jr.

"Don is out w kids all day, I'd like to see my favorite cousin," the text spread across my iPhone screen.

Kim and I were not actually cousins. We shared no blood. Our families had known one another for years. Our parents were best couple friends for decades. She and her brother and me and mine growing up living two houses away from one another on our parents' dead-end street. The busty, little lady and I had actually grown even closer in our twenties attending the same college. Then in our mid-thirties, we were pretty much besties, living only about a twenty-minute ride from one another across our big suburban town.

I fired back: "Time?"

"11:30. I'll be wearing my naughtiest panties and bra set, high heels, and have my new wooden spoon ready."

I didn't need to text 'WTF' as Kim would know this text would throw me for a loop as much as she knew, that I'd know, she was kidding. Sure, we had always flirted a good bit or more precisely, I flirted, and Kim simply chuckled at the innuendos. But beyond a requisite hug, and the lick-smack kiss we had been giving one another since we were teens and only managed when out of sight of family and friends, nothing sexual had occurred with us.

Mid-30's and holding, we had settled into twice-a-month lunches, taking in family wakes (which seemed to be coming too frequently as we grew older), and her inviting me by every other weekend or so for coffee and gossip. It wasn't so much that I hadn't imagined what her big boobs looked like naked, or hadn't fantasized landing a quick lip smack on each of her perfectly round big ass cheeks. But beyond a few sweet dreams I had about the lady over the years that had thrust me awake with a hard-on, I had never entertained any real hope of anything truly sexual happening with my cousin now that I was closer to her than I was with most actual family members.

And yeah, there was that married thing — I couldn't forget Don and the kids.

The short lady with the button nose and chestnut-colored curls and I were intimates in confidence and caring, and if anyone knew my penchant for spanking, it was my cousin-not-cousin. But the fevered imaginings I had related to Kim over the years, dates I told her about that had gotten bit kinky, even those moments when something would flitter across HBO that she'd text me about, all these were tidbits of my slight submissive sexual psyche Kim had always just accepted.

This latest text of hers simply came from a discussion we had just had about Kim's youngest, Jerry, selling some new promotion to raise money for a club at school. Not needing the kitchen utensil pack Jerry's club was getting a cool twenty for — Kim wasn't really that dedicated of a cook, her old set of spatula, wooden spoon, etc., showed no signs of wear — still, being the supportive mom that she was, she had plunked down the dollars to the cause.

"Yeah, yeah, I know how a housewife in her kitchen holding a wooden spoon turns you on," she quipped through a fast chuckle when we had discussed what her son had been selling just that past week.

Thus, she had bought the brand-new wooden spoon she was now teasing me with.

"Okay?" Kim texted/prodded.

"Yes, sure. Who wouldn't want to see you in panties and bra holding a wooden spoon?" I managed, playing along.

I got an emoticon smile in reply.

I received one last text as I was driving over to Kim's brick Tudor, telling me she had left the front door unlocked and would be waiting in her bedroom. Certainly, it was arousing to imagine Kim in matching lacey bra and panties, wearing at least three-inch black heels, holding that large new wooden spoon in one hand — or, better yet, smacking the ladle into her other hand — a huge smile playing across her pretty, slightly chubby face. The most revealing outfit I had ever seen on the thickly-built woman was a one-piece bathing suit, imagining Kim in lingerie was a nice fantasy to consider. Her dressed as she had teased she would be a mind-noodle I figured I'd keep locked and loaded this day, while Kim most likely would welcome me in her usual loose jeans and oversized sweater, a sure picture I'd be able to imagine later when I jerked-off tonight.

The usually noisy house was certainly quiet as I pushed open the door, shouted a "hello," and then began stepping down the hallway to my left as loudly as I could. I began talking to myself.

"Well, well, an empty house. What's gonna happen here?"

I kept walking.

"I hope that wooden spoon is strong."

I figured Kim'd be sitting on her bed laughing when I got to her, hoping she had fucked with my head even in the slightest... which she was, actually.

"Hi," my cuz said when I spun into her big brown-and-peach bedroom.

Seeing Kim dressed as she described she would be, sitting with knees poised tightly together at the edge of her bed, smiling wide and that damn spoon to her side, I came up short in the doorway, my mouth wide open and I am sure, my eyes popping out of my skull.

"Thought I was joking?" she said, not turning completely to me but resting her pretty chin on her left shoulder and leveling with a cool overly coy stare.

"Come on, come on... it's as much about you getting a good look as anything else."

I somehow managed to move my legs, took those few steps across the floor, and came to stand before her.

Holy s...h...i...t!

I ran my eyes up from up what had to be at least three-inch black heels, Kim's magnificent bulging calf muscles — muscles she always complained about, but I always thought very sexy (no cankle here, to be sure) — up her thick so-smooth bare thighs, to the tucked-in covered pretty blue deep 'V' I could just spy, up to her tummy — maybe not an intended surface or a six-pack, but again certainly trim and nowhere near the size she complained it always was — up to those magnificent big boobs obviously held high in underwire cups, to her long warm-looking neck and chin and then to her smile and deep brown-eyed gaze. I got all of the girl in one lascivious peek, her olive complexion alight in the light blue of her sky-blue panty and bra set.

She looked delicious.

"That was… obvious."

"You told me to look."

"It's unnerving to have you give me the once over. You're not gonna like it when I do it to you."

Before I could reply, she issued a command.

"Strip, all the way, completely, take every stitch of clothing off, this has been a long time coming, and we are gonna do this right."

How could I refuse? Why would I have wanted to?

Pinning my eyes to Kim's, I flipped off my sneakers, toe to heel, unzipped, threw off my t-shirt, then bent to rip my jeans down my legs and kicked them to the side of us onto my sneakers. My cock was just about tenting my jockeys. I gave her one big smile. She returned it, then I bent to strip my underwear down. My dick popping free, just about in Kim's face, I stood not a foot from her, just in my socks as she turned to me fully. The rush of being suddenly naked in front of this woman I had known for so many years nearly made me swoon. Feeling vulnerable, but at the same time so free, getting hard, finally able to relate to this lady on this level, and Kim seeming to like what she was then staring at, got me all warm and tingly.

I was aching to have her touch me and let me touch her.

"Mmmm," Kim ran her eyes up and down me quickly, then wiggled backward to get more of herself up on the bed. Sitting then really with just her heels dangling off the edge, she picked up the spoon.

"You really want this? To get across me, feel this spoon smacking your ass?"

'Oh yeah, the spanking,' I thought to myself. I had nearly forgotten.

I can't say I had ever really had any specific scenario in mind when I fantasized about being spanked. Yes, I had been on the receiving end of various women taking hand, belt, and yes, spoon to me a handful of times in my life. Save for one instance, though, the ladies who got me across or agreed to swat me as I bent before them, had done so all too quickly and never because they really wanted to, beyond hoping to give me a thrill.

Certainly, no woman in my past had ever managed such a premeditated consideration, and to have that woman be Kim, the sudden protagonist to my deepest fantasy, and seemingly so willing, was blowing my mind.

"Help me to understand, Jeremy, understand why this all gets to you like this."

"Well, you do look hot as hell!"

"I mean, the spanking, wanting to be across my knee, getting hit with a wooden spoon."

Certainly, this was an odd conversation to be having with me bare-assed naked and erect, standing over my cousin in stop-traffic-arousing lingerie. God knew, I wanted to just lunge across her, wiggle my tight little ass in her face and let her go to town on my cheeks. But the one thing about this fantasy of mine, and probably something Kim could sense, was that I liked talking about getting spanked as much as I did actually like being spanked.

"Like I told you many times, it's always just been a fantasy of mine."

"A nice lady sitting here in lingerie, tapping a hairbrush or a wooden spoon in the palm of her hand..." she said, smiled, and began to do just that, tap the spoon's little blonde-colored ladle into the palm of her right hand.

I tried not to swoon.

"Yea. Yeah, something like that."

"And only over my knee? You never think of any other positions?"

"I...uh..." I said, trying so hard not to take myself in hand over both Kim's actual undressed presence and what she was pulling out of me. I couldn't tell if she was just teasing me, generally curious, or both (I was sure it was both) as I tried to as much look at her pretty little brown eyes, as down her bulging cleavage, as to her bare legs.

"There are lots of positions," I continued and attempted to push my pelvis slightly forward to get her eyes off mine and down to my cock. Kim hadn't yet really given me more than a passing glance, and I was damn determined to get her to look at my popping dick.

"Wanna touch it, huh?" she said.

"I want you to."

"You know I can't."

"Figured, yeah."

"But maybe..." she said and scooted her bottom down her bedspread so she had her heels flush to the floor again. This time,

Kim spread her legs as I tried with all my might not to stare at her crotch.

"Put it right here," she said, patting her left knee.

I guess I kind of knew what she was asking, but it seemed so bizarre coming from this lady. Although, all that Kim was saying... and allowing and showing me right then was pretty fucking bizarre.

"Go ahead, just lay it right here on my knee."

I took two steps, grabbed my cock, and laid the head of my erection down on Kim's knee.

"Now," she continued, smiling at me widely.

Then, she crossed her right leg over her left, capturing the head of my dick between her knees. I had to adjust to keep from falling out, clutched as we were. I could all too easily slip free of Kim's knee hold if I worked at it. I knew, but I damn well wanted to stay standing tight to her, feeling that glorious warmth on top of my shaft.

"Now explain," she said, looking at me, those beautiful deep-set eyes truly full of concern.

I didn't need any further inducement than this wonderful woman's seeming interest and the leg lock she had on my cock. I stood up as close to Kim as I could without lying across her knee altogether, pushed myself forward for a better purchase between the underside 'cup' of her knee and the top of the one under me and began to explain the whole complicated mess of what I ached for and how it informed who I was.

I couldn't exactly recall the exact moment when my spanking fantasy had begun. Still, I knew I had connected it deeply to my libido since I was aware of my libido. It had never slaked, even when I had been lucky to find a woman or two to spank me. Relating this as I stood there locked between my cousin's knees was surely interesting (and arousing), and if my brief admission was all she'd allow. I poured my heart out as she sat under me in bra, high-cut panty and heels as I tried my best not to fuck her legs.

I would consider this late Sunday morning rendezvous an utterly satisfying experience. It wasn't every day I got to talk about my kink, saw my cousin undressed in such arousing underthings, or that I got to strip for her and rub my cock against her, even for the little amount she was allowing. I did have hope that since we had come this far, Kim might release me soon enough and get me across her lap or up on her bed and bounce that damn spoon across my ass. But I was well into the plus column right then even if nothing more happened between us.

Still, I made my explanation brief, ending with: "I guess it's a little different, maybe yes, kinky, and it's not all I want when it comes to sex. But I do like a confident, sexy lady giving me a little ass warming and a light scolding if she has a mind to. Especially if she is into it."

"I guess that makes sense," Kim said, lifted her knee off my cock and sat back on the bed again. Released, I stepped back to wag myself in her face again as she decidedly looked down at my dick for a good few seconds.

"I just had to know that it wasn't about the pain, ya know?" she said, looking at me then.

"Well, the spanking is no good for me unless it hurts," I said. "But no, I'm not a classic masochist in that sense. I don't get off on the pain."

"Yeah, I wouldn't be into that."

"I'm kinda surprised you are into any of this."

"Yeah, me, too."

"Ok, you can get up and over now," she added.

I didn't need any more urging, practically jumping across Kim's warm creamy lap and lying my chest across the top of her bed as she eased back and let me get into the most comfortable position I could while draping myself across her. I wiggled to fit my hard-on between her legs, Kim scooting forward ever so slightly and closing her thighs just enough so I could feel her sweet, thick warmth but not couldn't actually start rubbing in earnest.

"SHASMIT," the spoon's back said as my cousin landed her first smack.

I have read about 'subspace,' that floaty euphoric feeling some subs experience through pain, positioning, being bound, or working through a role-play scenario. But I had never experienced this, nor did I care to. My needs weren't so deep, weren't so kinky even. I just liked to have my tight, hairy buns swatted, hear the sound of whatever was spanking me bouncing off my cheeks, feel the sting it makes, maybe endure a little light scolding, feel my cock pound, but mainly have the spanking come from some real place of interest from the woman spanking me, and if I could dream it, maybe bring her some arousal.

"SNIPPA, SNIP," Kim flicked her wrist right about just where the very bottom of my right cheek folded into the back of my thigh. I wasn't sure if my cousin was aware of what smacking this spot would produce or if she had just accidentally hit me there, but the connection did cause me to clench, give a sharp yelp and push into her meaty thigh even more.

"SPA, SAP," Kim landed dead center cheek to cheek.

"Good?" she asked softly.

"Ya… yeah," I sighed.

I felt her sit back then as she stopped, laying her hand on my left ass cheek and managing a few quick deep inhales. Looking over my right shoulder, I watched my cousin's smile spread between her decidedly blushed cheeks.

"It's definitely interesting, that's for sure," she began. "But really, I'm not hitting hard, right? I mean I…"

"The smack under my cheek, top of my leg, that hurt."

"Here?" she asked and began to rub that soft spot she had hit just a minute before. Balancing my forearm on the bed, I looked back even further at the pretty lady.

"Yeah, there, there."

We both laughed as Kim placed the spoon to her side and began to massage all of my ass. I couldn't help but fall back across the bed as she kneaded and rolled my flesh. Certainly, we had never been in such a position, nor had she ever touched me quite like this. Of course, I loved the attention, the almost absentminded way she tickled and teased my hot skin as she began to give forth.

"I never thought about this, ever. Certainly, never seeing you naked."

"I kinda… I kinda figured," I said, trying not to start really humping her leg. She was raising a sure warmth to my flanks, and I was growing ever harder under her attention.

"But…" and here my cousin popped her pelvis up into me and giggled. "This is kinda hot, right?"

"Definitely."

"Once I got the idea of dressing for you, teasing you with the spoon, and then Don said he wanted to take the boys out to see that tractor pull, I knew I had to do this."

"SMIT, SMIT."

She landed one smack to each of the cheeks. Kim rained four more down side to side.

"SMIT, SMIT, SMIT, SMIT."

"I'm…" I said, pressing down into her as I couldn't hold myself back after the massaging and now the hand swatting. "I'm glad you did."

"Yeah, I can feel how glad," she said and closed her legs around my cock as I mustered all my will not to start pumping into the tight, warm, fleshy space Kim was creating with her thighs.

I wasn't about to ask why, from how long she had known me and my desire for spanking, that this was the day my cousin had decided to take advantage of being alone to do something I knew was well out of her wheelhouse. And, if, we'd have another moment like this ever again. I was just happy to be across Kim, enjoying her interest, attention and warmth. Had all of this been prompted by the new spoon she had acquired? Could something so simple push a woman like Kim to turn on a dime and manage such a premeditated moment?

"Hold on," she said and as I managed to get my right arm behind her back I felt Kim reach and "SMAT, SMAT, SMAT, SMAT, SMAT, SMAT, SMAT, SMAT, SMAT" my ass then spit a "and ten" at me, then "SMAT" bounced one last high stinging brush back smack off my right side.

"Okay, enough," Kim said, pushing me to roll off her lap.

I crumbled to the floor right up next to what I could surely then see were indeed three-inch black pumps.

"Fuck, I need an iced tea," she said, stepping over me. "Maybe a drink, even."

I managed to my knees to watch Kim's magnificent wide rear, the fleshy round expanse of it I couldn't appreciate until then, as she walked to her dresser drawer. Standing as best I could, I reached for my clothes, and we dressed in silence, me behind my cousin, as a slice of sunlight managed through her high bedroom window and that damn wooden spoon lying in a splash of light on her bed. I fumbled as much with my erection as over the fact that I was going to take every last second I could watching Kim wiggle her curvy bubble buns in her high-cut blue panties with their lace around the edges slip up and away into her jeans.

"We only ever talk about this in here," my cousin said, turning to me, then leaning in to kiss my mouth.

Her lips lingered longer than they ever had, almost to the point where I thought we were going to open our mouths, but then Kim was off me, lifting her hands to give her breasts a squeeze.

"And I'm not even sure we will be in here to do that again," she continued, giving me another one of her deep knowing stares. "But that was hot, Jeremy, fucking hot."

My cousin spun from me and out of the room as I followed. Seconds later I was standing in her kitchen, extricating the pod I wanted for our Sunday morning coffee clutch around her butcher block kitchen table, for yet another visit with my cousin Kim.

Lap Dance

By Aravielle

Kenny and I turned toxic eventually, but it wasn't always like that. By the end of our relationship I had become somebody that I didn't recognize. I was jealous, paranoid, accusatory and completely insecure. I now know that when you do not feel secure in yourself, your mind can do cruel things. You doubt everything: what you look like, what you're capable of, if you eat right, if you communicate well. It is consumption of the most devastating variety. I knew it peripherally then, but that lesson is etched in stone now. I had to cause an immense amount of pain to myself and to people I loved to learn that lesson. I won't soon forget. I hope not ever.

One night Kenny and his friends had gone out to a strip club. I never really cared about that sort of thing; it doesn't bother me. When Kenny came home he was primed! I said a silent thank you to whatever lovely young lady did my heavy lifting that day, and then proceeded to ask Kenny to go wash off the perfume and immense amount of body makeup that was all over him. Lap dances can get messy. I gestured up and down to him with a look of incredulity on my face as if I was presenting a disastrous scene to him. He had no idea what a state he was in. It wound up being a great night between us.

I have two distinct parts of our story — Kenny and I. The amazing growth and the utter destruction. I guess that's what made it good.

Bolt of Blue

By J.Z. Sharpe

Whenever the shop door opens, a small bell chimes. This causes the proprietor, an ancient woman with grizzled hair wrapped in a bun, to look up over her half-glasses. The usual garment district types always know what they want, and ask for it right away: wool gabardine with a subtle stripe (but not too subtle), velvet in varying shades of green (nothing too light), sequins to match a certain print (here's a swatch of it). But this man just stands there and blinks at all the bolts of fabric, so many piled from floor to ceiling in a space so narrow, one can touch both sides of the room without even trying. He seems stunned, as first-time customers often are.

"May I help you?" the woman asks.

The man looks at her with wide eyes, perhaps a little startled to see her face pop up from behind the counter, like a wren peeking out from a birdhouse.

"I want some silk," he blurts out. "Some Chinese silk."

"What color?"

"Oh, I'm not particular..." His words fade as he walks toward her, his fingers rushing some of the longer rolls. "Blue would be good, I think."

"And what will you be using it for?"

The man doesn't answer, too busy fingering a bit of brocade the color of fresh celery.

"Pardon?" he says at last.

"What will this be used for? Clothing, or interior decoration? Are you looking for something upholstery weight, or lighter?"

"It will be worn by a friend of mine, a woman." A smile breaks out from under his dark beard for just a moment, the way the sun might make a brief showing on a cloudy day. "It should wrap well."

"I see." The woman rises from her stool and shuffles past her wares, mentally paging through her inventory. "Up there, I have a lovely blue pattern. See it? Let me get it down for you."

"Can I help?"

She waves him away. A regular wouldn't even bother to ask. They would simply step aside while she wielded the long metal rod that pulls the bolts down from their perches, the way she has done for thirty-five years, with the strength and agility of a woman half her age. The shimmering roll drops between them, and the man runs his palm along its smooth surface. A pattern of leaves and vines is woven into the cloth.

"Beautiful," he whispers. "It's perfect."

Then he reaches into his inside pocket and brings out a leather-bound checkbook.

"Oh, no, I'm sorry," the woman clucks. "No checks. Only cash."

From someone she knew, she would take a check without question. But she has never seen this man before, and nowadays one must be careful.

Fortunately, her request doesn't faze him at all. He reaches into a different pocket and produces a wallet.

"How much?"

She quotes the price and holds her breath. This silk is fifty dollars a yard, and it's nearly a full bolt. Surely, he doesn't carry that much cash? Many of her regular customers couldn't afford something so dear, and in New York, only a fool would walk around with money like that.

Yet he surprises her by laying out a row of crisp bills on her counter top.

"I'm sorry," he says. "I have nothing smaller than hundreds."

"That's fine," the woman replies, knowing that as soon as he leaves, she will have to close the shop a while to make an unscheduled bank deposit. She completes the sale in the old-fashioned way (no computerized cash register for her!), doing the arithmetic in her head and writing the numbers on a form, before tearing off one copy for the customer and keeping another for herself.

After the man leaves, she watches him walk toward Seventh Avenue, where he can be seen for only a few seconds before disappearing into the crowd.

He is not a tall man, yet he commands a certain presence as he moves with the grace of a leopard through the clusters of people coming the other way. The bolt of cloth, wrapped in protective brown paper, is like a scabbard, and she spies its top long after the man himself can't be seen. Sometimes the woman likes to imagine what will become of her wares: an evening gown for his beloved, perhaps? For some beauty who has lost her heart to him? She smiles as she looks for her bankbook, her own memories too strong and too sweet to be ignored.

* * * * *

When he gets to Seventh Avenue, he opens his cell phone with a swift flick of the wrist. Using the speed dial, he reaches her right away. No doubt Precious has been expecting his call, for she answers on the first ring.

"I'm on my way to the studio," he tells her.

"Yes, Sir. I'll meet you."

"Listen carefully. There are certain things I want you to do when you get there." He thinks he hears her breath catch as he says this, exactly the reaction he wanted. "First, turn on the answering machine, and shut off its speaker."

"Yes, Sir."

"When I arrive, I want to find you naked, standing with your back to the door, your feet together, your hands behind your back."

"Naked, Sir? No shoes?"

"No, not even shoes. Entirely naked. And silenced, gagged with your panties in your mouth."

He hears her swallow. "Yes, Sir."

"Not a thread showing. Is that understood, Precious?"

"Yes, Sir. Naked with my back to the door, hands behind my back and panties in my mouth."

"Left wrist in your right hand."

"Yes, Sir."

"Don't disappoint me."

"I… I won't, Sir."

He ends the call and smiles. Of course she won't, he thinks. She never does.

* * * * *

Precious has been waiting at least fifteen minutes, standing just the way he wants, naked with her hands behind her back. When he opens the door, he will see her pretty derriere right away, those rounds of flesh he loves to spank. He will see her long red hair, those strands he loves to grab in his fist when he kisses her. Where is he? What's keeping him? She listens to the faraway rumble of traffic, the lonely wail of an ambulance headed north. Her pussy quivers and moistens with anticipation.

At last! The jingle of keys, the squeal of that stubborn hinge as he opens the door. He laughs softly.

"Oh, Precious, you are so lovely."

Footsteps, and then he is there, standing in front of her with his dark eyes sliding up and down her naked form.

"Your panties are in your mouth, too. Very good." He taps his finger against her puffed-out cheek. "I have a present for you. Stay right here."

She hears the sound of paper tearing, then being crumpled and tossed aside. His mouth brushes her ear as he leans close and whispers.

"Put your feet together. I'm going to push something between your ankles and I want you to hold it there. Do you understand?"

She nods.

Precious feels him work something into that narrow space and glances down to see the end of a bolt of blue silk. The rest of it is held in her beloved's arms as he walks around her in a slow circle, wrapping her tight in layer after layer of cool fabric, first covering her shins, then her knees and thighs. For a moment, he pauses to touch the trimmed fur around her pussy, then wraps several layers extra tightly around her hips. The floor creaks in time to his dance. Now her arms are held in place, close to her sides, and her breasts are pressed flat against the weight of this glorious blue silk. He pauses to examine the layers and leaves a small opening where he can still tease her nipples, which rise furiously in reaction to his touch. A few more passes around her body and stopping at her shoulders, he is done. Two or three yards of fabric are left, which he cuts away with a pair of sturdy tailor's shears, securing the end with a handful of safety pins. As a finishing touch, he rips a narrow strip off the excess fabric and ties it around her mouth, pressing the panties against the back of her throat.

"A chrysalis," he says softly. "The advent of a butterfly, hiding her beauty from the world until she is ready to fly."

His fingers wriggle under the cloth to pinch her left nipple, making Precious sigh.

Now he asks her to lie down on the floor, and tries to help her kneel, or at least bend her knees slightly, but she is wrapped too tightly. Oh dear, she thinks, suppressing a giggle. What a predicament! She sways, but just as she feels herself in danger of toppling, he grabs her around the hips and tosses her over his shoulder in the classic fireman's hoist. He takes a few steps across the room and drops her onto the bed, an activity that brings her giggles to the surface, and makes him laugh, too, if only for a second.

Then his face grows serious again, as his hands travel over her silk-covered form, lingering on her hips, her thighs, and her confined pussy.

Precious can't help but lose herself in the chaos of new sensation. Being so confined so tightly, with her arms pressed against her back and her legs bound together, every breath is a reminder of the cocoon of blue silk that renders her helpless. She's a little scared, as she always is when he tries something new — yet she also feels safe, swaddled in the smooth warmth of the silk. His stern eyes study every inch of her, from her clenched toes to the length of her bare neck, which he laces with kisses.

"My beautiful butterfly," he whispers. "I'm going to make you fly."

He picks up the shears. Will he set her free? She considers this possibility with mixed emotions, not sure she is ready to leave this sweet enclosure. Fortunately, he's not ready to let her out. Instead, he snips away at the silk between her legs, until he makes a hole large enough for exploration.

"Precious!" he says, holding up his fingertips, now shiny with her moisture. "Do you have any idea how wet you are, my dear? You're like some pretty little bonbon, lovely to look at, and with a sweet center, too."

He licks away the juices.

"Delicious," he sighs and goes back for more.

Precious closes her eyes and concentrates on the way his fingers dance with such skill, despite the constraints of the silk. She strains against the binding, raising her hips off the bed and pressing into his eager hand. Let me fly, she keeps thinking. Just don't release me! It feels too good inside here.

All too soon, she trembles and the entire length of her bound body stiffens, as the force of the orgasm races down her spine. Even now his hand doesn't stop; it remains buried in the depths of her secret flower.

"Yes, you like this, don't you, my dear?"

He seems so pleased, as he always does when she climaxes, and he has found another way to bind her to him.

"Go ahead, let it go. I won't tell you to stop."

Bound so tightly, so safe, so hot — she does as he says, and she keeps on coming, riding the waves, until her eyes fall shut and she drifts off to sleep.

* * * * *

When Precious awakes, she is saddened to find the cocoon gone, and the gag removed. She stretches, spreading her arms like wings, and smiles. Then she raises her head to see her beloved sitting in a nearby chair, the remains of the silk folded neatly in his lap. The first light of day is shining through the window behind him.

"You enjoyed that?" he asks.

She nods. "Where did you find such lovely fabric?"

"Some hole-in-the-wall, down in the garment district."

"It's so beautiful. I hope you didn't rip it all getting me out."

"No, my dear, I was careful not to do that."

He laughs and goes to sit next to her on the bed, where he lays the bundle of cloth between them. She smiles as he touches her cheek.

"After all, we just might do this again. Would you like that?"

Precious doesn't say a word — but then, she doesn't need to speak. Her eager eyes say it all.

THEMES: ass play, bedtime routine, breasts, breast play, cock worship, dominance/submission, inspection, orgasm control, protocol

Wednesday and Friday

By Olivia

Five nights a week, she got herself ready for bed, just like anyone would. Okay, it was a little bit different for her because she was required to write in her journal. She could write about anything she wanted, but her work needed to include certain elements. She needed to complete the page where she recorded any infractions of rules, and the page where she recorded progress on her goals. Other than that, she would take a quick shower, lotion her body, and meditate for at least 20 minutes.

Then she would text Sir that she was ready for bed. After sending the text, she would kneel, still naked from her shower. She kept a comfortable chair in her bedroom, next to her bed, that was just for him. She would kneel by the right side of the chair and wait.

Usually, he came to her room shortly after she had sent the text. Occasionally, he would be busy and she'd have to wait a while. But most nights, she only knelt waiting for five or 10 minutes. During that time, she was supposed to prepare to talk about any of the mundane details of their days — plans, problems, or things she appreciated — the conversations most couples would have.

Except she would be kneeling at his feet while they had the conversation. Naked. They had followed this routine for a while, and it seemed quite natural to her. She knew that she also needed to spend a few minutes thinking about her submission to him. Any issues could be recorded in the journal and shared at the appropriate time, but he also liked to know that the nature of their relationship was on her mind.

Tonight was Tuesday, and as she knelt, waiting for him to join her, she wondered what he would want from her tonight. Usually, he spent 30 to 45 minutes with her before he put her to bed. Sometimes he just sat with her, stroking her hair while they talked. Other times, he would allow her to use her mouth to please him.

She smiled to herself as she thought that. Wondered when she had started thinking about it that way, as she thought those words, "allow her to use her mouth to please him." She remembered the training she had undergone. The hours she had spent with his cock in her mouth, learning all the ways he liked. Practicing every day, sometimes two or three times a day, until he was sure that she could please him adequately. She almost laughed, what an odd life I have, she thought.

But she remembered her pleasure when he told her she had passed her training. Thinking about it now made her long to taste him tonight. 'But I'm not sure I'll be allowed to,' she thought. She shook her head, remembering men before Sir who had longed for her to suck their dick, and times that she had refused them.

She had been waiting with eyes downcast, but suddenly sensed movement. Looking up, she saw Sir standing in the doorway, watching her. As their eyes met, she smiled, delighted to see him. When he smiled back, she felt like the whole room lit up.

He was carrying a cup of tea and a bottle of water. He set them down on the nightstand, then looked down at her.

"Sweet sub girl," he said, and her smile grew. He settled into his chair.

"Good girl," he said, stroking her head with one hand. "Everything okay today?"

"Yes, Sir," she said. "Everything's good."

And it had been, or she wouldn't have said that. The penalty for polite lies was not one she wanted to pay.

He grasped her hair tightly at the nape of her neck.

"Up," he said.

He released her then and she stood on her own.

"Prepare for inspection," he said.

Surprised, she moved into the first position, with her legs spread wide, hands laced together behind her head. She had not expected this, but she thought she was as well prepared as she could be.

He stood, too, and turned on the flashlight on his phone. He began by shining the light on her ears, both inside and behind them, checking to make sure they were clean. This always made her smile a bit, she felt like a small child for this part of it.

Then he checked her nipples, "to make sure they were working," he'd said once. "They should get nice and hard, you should get turned on and wet, and at some point the inspection should hurt," he had explained. "That tells me you have healthy, well-functioning nipples."

Sometimes he started slowly, sucking and teasing them. Other times he used ice, or nipple clamps. Tonight, he used his fingers, playing with her gently at first, then twisting, tugging and pinching until she was whimpering.

"Are you hot? Wet?" he asked.

"Yes, Sir," she said, still a bit breathless. She was prepared for him to check, looking forward to it actually, but instead he moved around her, pulled a nearby ottoman up behind her.

"I want you on your back," he said. "Knees to your chest. I want to be able to see how wet you are."

She had practiced this before. It didn't take her long to take her place on the ottoman. Her head was comfortably supported, but her ass hung off the end a bit. By pulling her knees up hard against her chest, she achieved a nice balance and was quite comfortable. Physically anyhow.

Of course this gave him a clear view of her pussy and ass. He scooted the ottoman closer, but didn't touch her open thighs, her throbbing pussy or the smaller, puckered entrance. Instead, he sat back in his chair and tasted his tea.

There was silence for a maybe a minute. Then he spoke.

"I talked to Nora today about our plans for a dinner party. Are you still thinking four or five couples?"

"Yes, Sir," she said, flushing with humiliation.

"These are all folks in the kink community, right?"

"Yes, Sir. A couple of the women are also writers, and some of the Doms are starting a Kinky Retreat kind of thing."

"That sounds like fun," he said. "Do you want to have a play party afterwards? We could open up the dungeon, really get it back together again."

She hesitated a moment. It sounded like a great idea, but she knew she couldn't really think like this. She wanted his hands on her. She was open to pleasing him any way possible.

"Can't think, can you?" and she knew he was laughing.

Leaning forward, he used his thumbs to open her nether lips, leaving her clit exposed.

She whimpered. "No, Sir."

"That's okay, we can talk later. I just want to make sure your cunt is working right."

He stroked her clit.

"Don't cum now!" he commanded.

She knew that there was almost no chance of an orgasm for her on a Tuesday, so she was not surprised or disappointed.

He wet his finger in the juices from her pussy and slid it into her tight asshole, stopping at the first knuckle. She whimpered at the discomfort, then whimpered again when he withdrew it. He cleaned his finger with a wipe from the package on the nightstand beside him.

"You're a good girl," he said. "I want to feel your mouth on my cock. You may use the kneeling cushion."

She managed to get up not too ungracefully, grabbed the cushion, and began to settle herself in place on the floor in front of him. He was holding his cock in his hand, and she licked her lips in anticipation.

"Open your mouth," he said. "Put your tongue out. Farther. Now wait."

He continued stroking his cock while she waited obediently, longing to taste him. She didn't usually get to taste his cock until Wednesday or Friday.

A Day at the Museum

By J.Z. Sharpe

The bus let us off at the museum's front door. Will grabbed my hand as soon as we hit the sidewalk.

"Come on," he said with a grin. "I want to show you one of my favorite places in the whole city."

We flew right past the sculpture on the first floor, heading for the stairs that would take us to the mezzanine. The place was quiet, as one would expect on a Tuesday afternoon. Except for an occasional guard, we appeared to have the place all to ourselves.

"It's up here," Will said breathlessly. Then, he stopped. "Close your eyes. I want it to be a surprise."

I didn't like the sound of this. "How far do I have to go?"

"Just a few feet." He laughed. "Come on! I won't let you walk into anything."

So, I shut my eyes and let him take my hand in his and lead me to our destination. We turned once, twice, then finally came to a halt. Will took a deep breath, then exhaled with a sigh.

"Okay, you can look."

The painting before me monopolized the entire room, despite the distracting crimson wallpaper behind it, despite the ornate gilt frame that spoke of its value. A man of the 17th century, dressed in champagne-colored silk, stared back at me with dark brown eyes and a mischievous grin. The deep waves of a long black wig surrounded his angular face, and a narrow mustache grew under his long nose. His elbow rested on a stone wall behind him; birds flew across a sunset in the background. A small white dog, of an overactive breed that chews shoes and jumps up on strangers, sat attentively at his feet.

"Who's that?" I asked.

"Louis the XIV, I think. One of those famous French kings. Although I never paid much attention to who he really was, y'know?" Will put his arm around my waist and pulled me closer to him. "You know me. I prefer to use my imagination and make something up." He nodded toward a bench, a few feet away. "Come on, let's go spend some time with him, shall we?"

Even though we had plenty of room, Will cuddled up to me, close enough to press his hip against mine. His arm was still curled around my midsection, with his fingertips resting gently under my right breast. I felt like I sat in the audience of some strange play that was yet to begin, some arcane tableaux about a time in history unfamiliar to me. Classical music played overhead with the volume turned so low, I couldn't make it out well enough to place the name of the piece or its composer. It was meant more as architectural perfume, I'm sure, to cover the sounds of air conditioning and footsteps.

Will whispered into my left ear, his lips not even an inch from me. "So, Colleen, do you see him looking at you? Staring? Very intense, isn't he?"

"He's just a painting. Just oil and canvas. He's not a real person."

"No? He looks real enough to me. And he was a person at one time, remember." Will's hand slipped down to cup my ass, while he set his other one on my lap, dangerously close to the hem of my skirt. "He might be dead now, at least physically — but do we really know what lives on?"

"Oh, come on!" I laughed nervously. "Now you're spooking me out."

"Perhaps." His fingers curled around my skirt, the tips barely touching my nylons. "When I was a kid, I used to come here after school. Sometimes, I would talk to this guy."

"Did he ever talk back?"

"Sure! We had some fantastic conversations." In my lower peripheral vision, I could see his hand start to slip under my skirt. "He's quite a ladies man, you know."

"I see."

"He has great appreciation for beauty. Taught me everything I know." Will smiled at me, then turned to his friend. "This is the woman I was telling you about. Isn't she lovely?"

"You told him about me?" I shook my head. "Now I know you're nuts."

Will ignored me, preferring to trace his fingertips along the tops of my stockings. So this was why he wanted me to leave the panty hose behind today and wear garters instead. The skin of my inner thighs received every touch, no matter what its source, even the slightest movement of air. I felt my legs part involuntarily, which seemed to please Will quite a bit, if the smile on his face was any indication.

"Yes, she's quite passionate. How astute of you to notice, your majesty! Of course, you can probably see the evidence, can't you? She's getting quite wet down there, just the way a woman should be."

"I am?"

"Of course you are." He pressed three fingers against my pussy and I felt the chill from newly produced juices, not yet dry on my silk panties. This explained not only why he demanded the stockings and garters, but why he insisted that the panties would go on after the garter belt. I could feel him tugging at the elastic, and I snapped my thighs together again.

"Damn it, Will! Somebody could see!"

"No one will see us. No one's even here."

"A guard just walked by."

"Good, we'll have the place to ourselves for at least ten minutes now. I know their cycle. Once around the mezzanine, back through the water color gallery, with a quick peek into the stairwell. Remember, I've been hanging out here for ages." He started to massage me, a clockwise motion with my labia trapped in his fingertips. My thighs parted again, and I glanced up at the painting. The man did seem to be enjoying himself.

"Was he a flirt?" I asked, to distract myself from my increasing arousal.

"Good god, yes! One of the best." Will's touch continued, lifting me on its slow ascent to the stars. "Weren't you, your majesty? You just loved to see them squirm and sigh. Especially the pretty ones like her."

I threw back my head, letting out a low moan — then thought better of it, and straightened immediately. The guard was back now, hovering in the doorway with his hands behind his back.

Maybe he'd watch us for a second and if only we could just keep quiet, he'd go away.

But I couldn't possibly have such luck. The slow dirge of the guard's approaching footsteps slowed Will's ministrations and brought his hand out from beneath my clothing, although it only stopped as far as my hemline.

"Good afternoon," the guard said when he was only a few feet away. "Enjoying the exhibit?"

"Oh, yes, sir, very much," Will replied.

"That's quite a beauty." The guard nodded toward our oil-based observer. "You're in luck. It goes on loan to the Metropolitan Museum in New York soon."

"Really?" Will sounded truly surprised. "For how long?"

"At least a year, I think."

"Well then, we timed our visit well, didn't we, dear?"

I nodded. "Absolutely, darling."

He cocked his head toward me. "She loves art. Any kind of art. I try to indulge her every chance I get."

"That's very nice of you, sir." The guard smiled. "She must have good taste."

"Excellent taste. It's one of the things I love about her."

"Very good, sir." The guard's smile passed over to me as he turned on his heels and started for the door. "Well, I'll leave you to enjoy the exhibit. Remember, we close at five."

Will glanced at his watch. "Another hour then. Thanks."

I watched the guard continue on his rounds, from the gallery where we sat to the other side of the mezzanine.

"That was close," I said.

"Nonsense. They see this sort of thing all the time. Okay, where were we?" Will chuckled. "Oh, yes, of course. Thank you for reminding me, your majesty. I believe I was about to show you her precious womanly treasures. Spread your legs for me, would you, dear?"

"Right here? Now?"

"Colleen, he wants to see. Don't hide your beauty." Will nuzzled my ear. "I promised I'd show you off to an old friend. Please?"

I swung my knees apart, thinking the whole time — this is ridiculous. This man is not real. But I couldn't avoid the sensation of being watched, being studied and admired. His eyes were so dark, so richly amused. Will pushed my panties down and in one swift motion, had them around my ankles. "Oh, my god," I whispered, embarrassed.

"Lift your feet." I did as I was told, too surprised to resist. Will crumpled the panties in his fist, grinned at his friend the king, then stuffed them into my coat pocket. "You know, you're lucky I haven't stuffed these into your mouth," he said. "That's what he wants me to do."

"He sounds rather kinky."

"Oh, he is, he really is. He used to play these wonderful bondage games with his chambermaids. Told me about them in great detail once." Will reached down and fumbled in his pocket. "Yes, of course I brought it with me," he said to the king in the painting. "Let's give it a try, shall we?"

"Give what a try?" I asked with more than a little trepidation.

"This adorable little device." He held up his pointer finger and I saw a little plastic object, like a magic decoder ring, wrapped around his upper knuckle. "I found it on the Internet. You'd love the Internet, your majesty. A garden of earthly delights!"

I heard a little snap, followed by a hum. Then I felt that hum, gently floating up my thighs and over my nether lips. When it came too close to my clit, I jumped, which made Will laugh out loud.

"Feels too good, huh?"

"Wait — what is that — that thing?"

"A little vibrator. It's supposed to be the smallest in the world. Takes a hearing aid battery, that's how tiny it is." He pressed it against my pubic bone and nearly sent me sailing through the roof. "She likes it, your majesty! Such a shame you never had such devices in your day. I'm sure you could have put them to good use."

I brought my hand down on top of his, to guide him right to the place where I needed his touch the most. I'd forgotten all about his other hand until now, when he gave my left cheek a nice solid squeeze.

"Oooh, yes!" I cried. "Please don't stop!"

"Don't worry." Will cocked his head in the painting's direction. "He won't let me. Not until you come."

Through the hair that had fallen over my face, I looked up at the man in the champagne silk, who stared back at me with the eyes of amusement. I began to wonder about him and, more importantly, to wonder about the women who had loved him. There must have been a lot of them. He smiled at me, that curious, slightly lopsided expression that he must have shared with a large number of fortunate ladies. I smiled back. The waves of pleasure from Will's little toy rushed through me with increasing vigor, and

I really did hope that he would never stop, even after I came. I was sure that one orgasm would not be enough.

How wonderful you are, cherie, said a voice I didn't recognize. You are such a treasure, such a prize. Your sighs of passion are like music, and the scent of it! A rare perfume, like none I've encountered before! Close your eyes, lean back, let him touch you and bring you to that magical moment of climax. I only wish I could be the one to arouse you, for I could teach your friend a few tricks, yes I could. But he's doing quite well all on his own, nevertheless. What I wouldn't give for a taste of you, my love! How I would love to lay my tongue against your sweetest places, I'm sure you are quite delicious — and I have tasted some of the finest female delicacies, yes I have. But you, I'm sure, would be more luscious than any of them. Oh, I hear your breath getting faster, I see a blush gathering on your cheeks. You want to come, don't you? Yes, you want your sensual reward. So what is stopping you, cherie? Is it because you're out in public, in the middle of an art museum? There is no one around to see this. No one here except for you, and your lover — and of course, me. Come, my dear. Do it for me.

"Yes… you…" I whispered. "Your majesty…"

Will kissed my cheek. "Is he talking to you now?"

"Maybe…"

I wriggled my ass against Will's palm, trying to stay in sync with the buzzing toy. The orgasm began as a warm glow, then grew to a fire that nearly consumed me. I clutched the bench with my hands and ground my pussy into Will's hand.

"Yes! Yes! Please! Oh — so wonderful!"

My thighs slammed together, trapping poor Will between them, right up to his wrist (not that he complained, mind you). I froze, desperate to seize the moment and determined to never let it go.

"Yes… yes… thank you… oh, yes… so, so good…"

"Shh, we're not alone."

I looked over Will's shoulder. Two elderly women had come in through the far door, clutching guidebooks and chattering in high, enthusiastic voices.

"It's incredible, Margaret!" crowed the taller one. "I haven't seen a collection like this since we were in France."

"Just sit up and try to look like nothing's going on," Will said under his breath. I tried to hide my face under my hair, for I'm sure it was as scarlet as the flocked wallpaper behind the king's portrait. It certainly felt warm enough to be so red. "Do you need to go freshen up?"

"Yeah, that's a good idea. Which way to the rest rooms?"

"Through that door and to the left."

I stood on shaky legs and held the back of the bench for a moment, in a feeble attempt to regain my balance. The two women stopped at several other paintings, but barely looked at the king. I'm sure they didn't know what they were missing. After a few minutes, they shuffled on to the next gallery, gabbing non-stop as they went.

"Your panties are in your pocket," Will said. "In case you want them."

I felt their silkiness with my fingertips. "Of course. Thanks."

"No problem. Take your time."

As I left the room, I heard Will laugh and say something out loud, and I could have sworn that I heard another man reply — in a French accent.

* * * * *

When I came out of the ladies room, Will was right outside, leaning against the wall, waiting for me.

"Ready to go?" he asked. "They're closing in fifteen minutes. I thought you might like to go get a drink."

"That sounds like a great idea. I could use one."

He put his hand on my elbow and started to lead me toward the stairs, but I stopped him. "Could we go back and see the painting one more time?"

"What, the portrait of the king?"

"If you wouldn't mind? Just one more look."

"Of course. I don't mind in the least."

I stood in the doorway and just studied the painting (I didn't have time to go back in for a closer look). For several precious minutes, I stared at the tall, slender man in his archaic dress and that cumbersome wig, with the little dog at his feet, the waning hours of the day as a backdrop. It's just a painting, I reminded myself. Just a lot of oil and pigment on old canvas, trapped in a gold leaf frame and imprisoned in a climate-controlled art gallery. Nothing about it is alive.

But as I turned to go, I heard a throat clearing. I looked at the king, right into his strong and handsome face. I can't say for sure, of course — but I could have sworn I saw him smile — and with a flirtatious twinkle in his handsome eyes, he winked, right at me.

THEMES: ass play, bondage, breast play, breasts, dominance/submission, fingering, inspection, sharing, training

The Trainer

By Olivia

"May I touch?" he asks.

It is my body he's talking about, but he's not asking for permission from me. He's asking the man who has put me in this situation. He nods.

"Of course," he says.

I say he had put me in this situation, and that is partly true, but I have also set myself up for this.

His name is Dylan, after the author not the singer, and he is my Dom. Or maybe my Master and we just haven't said it yet, I don't know. But it is mostly his fault that I'm standing here naked in front of some man I don't even know. Some man who is going to touch me.

I watch this man move closer to me and I might step back if I could, but I'm in cuffs, ankles and wrist, held in place by leather strips that attach to rings set in the floor for my ankles and leather straps dangling from the ceiling for my wrists. My legs are spread open so he will have easy access to all parts of me.

He touches my breast. My left breast, lifting it on his palm as if weighing it. Then, his licks his thumb before it lands on my nipple, which is already getting hard, thrusting forward as if asking for attention. His thumb barely makes contact with the nipple. He touches it gently and then pulls back, holding his thumb about a half inch away.

To my shame, before I can even think, much less stop myself, I have thrust my breast forward, the nipple reaching his thumb. Apparently that nipple does indeed want attention. I blush, and he laughs, moving his hand away. Heat rushes through my body, embarrassment, shame, and arousal mixing to make me squirm and my pussy throb.

He turns to Dylan.

"She responds nicely. What have you taught her?"

Dylan shakes his head.

"Not much. She's naturally submissive, good with her mouth, and enjoys obeying. Gets hot easy. She loves being tied up, likes a good hard spanking. I haven't trained her at all, just enjoyed her natural talents."

Without warning, the man moves back toward me, one hand goes between my thighs and penetrates me so suddenly that I cry out. He probes with his finger, exploring the hot, wetness at my core. He withdraws the finger just as quickly and a whimper escapes me. He grins.

"Have you fucked her ass?" He asks, and I blush again.

"No," Dylan shrugs, "it's not a big thing for me."

The man steps behind me, with one hand on my back, he pushes 'til I bend at the waist, pressing me as far as I can go within my restraints. With both hands, he spreads my cheeks, exposing the tiny puckered entrance to the narrow passage.

Then, he moves one hand away and I'm holding my breath, expecting pain, but he doesn't penetrate me. He just touches me there, circles the little opening with his finger.

I hear myself making little sounds, little whimpers, moving my hips as if seeking more contact. Another rush of shame rips through me.

With one hand on my shoulder, he indicates I should stand up again. I feel a little dizzy. This is a lot to absorb.

"Virgin," he says, "Or just really tight. If she's been used there before, it was a long time ago."

I'm suddenly aware that he's really not talking to me, he's asking Dylan questions and talking to him as if... and it hits me hard, as if... as if something, only then I don't have words for it. What? As if I can't talk, as if Dylan talks for... talks for me. And oh, my, I sway on my feet, what have I done here? I feel a bit panicky. And dizzy. What the fuck have I done?

*　*　*　*　*

There is a flurry of movement around me, an arm around my waist, and his voice in my ear, "Sit."

When I hesitate, he says it again, pressing down on my shoulder with the other hand.

"Sit now."

I bend at the knees, thinking I'm going to fall, but there is a chair behind me, so I land on that instead. Because of the way I had been bound, I am sitting with my knees positioned wide open, I can feel the texture of the chair, cool and smooth, against the lower lips of my pussy. My wrists had been attached to leather straps but held at waist level, they are raised now, almost above my head. But I am sitting, and not so dizzy, my breathing is slower.

Gratefully, I say, "thank you."

He glances at me, but doesn't respond. To Dylan, he says, "How did you decide to bring her here? What did you tell her to expect?"

Dylan looks away and I know he's embarrassed. I've seen that look before when he's done something he's not proud of. It worries me.

"Well," he says, "I met her at the club. We've been dating and playing a little bit, she's really into submission and I like being a Dom, so we've been getting along real good. But she wants to go deeper with it, and I don't really know if I do. But I didn't want to let her down. So I told her there was this man who trains subs and did she want to try that? I called and set up an appointment and here we are."

He shrugs. I listen to this and tears well up, but then anger is right behind that. I don't know if I want to break down and sob, or break free and kill Dylan.

The man seems pretty angry, too. Without taking his eyes off Dylan, he unfastens the links on my wrists so my hands are free.

To Dylan, he says, in the coldest tones I'd ever heard, "So essentially you brought her here without a clue. You didn't know what you were doing, so instead of informed consent, she's been blindsided. Did you follow any of the preparation directions?"

"Preparation?" Dylan sounds baffled.

I sigh because that doesn't really surprise me.

"Oh, in that email you sent," he says. "Yeah, I saw that, well, I didn't really have a chance to–"

"Stop."

The man takes one step closer to Dylan, who backs up two steps.

"You've broken our agreement. Out. Now."

Dylan hesitates, looking at me. "Leave? Ok, I guess… But — shouldn't she come with me? And do I get a refund?"

The man laughs, completely without humor.

"No," he says. "No she shouldn't go with you. I'm not kicking her out, just you. And no, you don't get a refund. I guess you 'didn't get a chance' to read the non-refundable clause in the contract either. Go."

Dylan looks at me like he expects me to say something, but I just look away.

"Baby," he says, "I didn't see things going this way, I'm real sorry, but it looks like I gotta go. You okay?"

I've heard this line before, so I don't even look at him, don't give any sign I even heard him. I mean, I'm sitting here naked with a stranger and he's leaving me here, how the hell would anything about that be okay?

"OK," he says. "I guess I'll see you later."

And the bastard leaves.

The man, whose name I still don't know, takes an afghan from the couch and drapes it around me. It feels warm and reassuring and a few of the tears in my eyes spill over. He pulls a chair closer, turns it so the back is facing me, and straddles the chair.

"So," he says. "First of all, if you want to leave now, just tell me. I'll give you your clothes, of course, and pay for an Uber to take you home."

I almost nod, yes, I should just go home and die of shame. But his eyes are kind and I had been looking forward to this so much...

"Or..." he says, "you can stay. Experience what it would be like to train as a submissive with me. He's already paid for a week, you are welcome to use the time."

Sitting there, naked underneath the afghan he's wrapped around me, my ankle cuffs still attached to rings in the floor, ensuring that my knees are wide open, with a man whose name I don't even know, I can't believe I'm thinking about staying. Training as a submissive... Am I out of my mind? I open my mouth to tell him I want to go home, but... I'm surprised by what I hear come out.

"I don't know," I say. "I don't know. I think I should go home, But..."

He is watching me, no sign of impatience, just watching me.

"But I guess... I guess I don't really want to. I mean. I took a week off work for this. And... And I know it's stupid, but I really, really wanted to do this."

He nods.

"And you can do it, if you still want to. As long as you don't let Dylan..." but he stops there and shakes his head. "Never mind that. Let's talk about what I offer in submissive training and what you want."

He pauses.

"I am going to unfasten the straps on your ankles so you can feel the freedom and the weight of your own choice."

He is on one knee before me, unfastening the straps from the cuffs. I am very aware of his body, so close. His hand brushes my leg and I swallow hard. When he is done, he settles back on the chair. I am still wearing the cuffs, but they are no longer attached to anything. Still naked, covered only by the afghan.

"I don't even know your name!" I explode.

That pushes me over the edge. I burst into tears.

I cry, tears running down my face, holding the afghan tightly around me. All the disappointment of the day, and the shame of how this day has gone, are overwhelming.

The unnamed man watches me for a moment. Then he stands, turns the chair around so it's facing the right way, and sits.

"Come here, girl," he says.

Startled, I stand. I move toward him, not sure in that moment what he wants me to do.

"Kneel, right here," he says, motioning to the floor in front of him.

Without thinking, I go down to my knees in front of him. He touches my shoulders, letting me lean into him. I rest my head on his lap and sob.

When I am all cried out, and have used up his Kleenex, I sigh. The last sob has left me. I'm tired, drained of emotion, and suddenly very aware that I am kneeling in front of this man as if… I pull back.

"Good girl," he says.

I grin at him.

"Thank you, Sir," I say, feeling just a bit flirty, and even a bit submissive. But also feeling a bit more myself. "So what have I gotten myself into here? And, um, what should I call you?"

He smiled at me, his green eyes warm and interested.

"Training school," he says. "That's what you've gotten yourself into, although there is still a way out if you want it. And I'm Benjamin Hendrix, Ben to my friends. You may call me, Sir Ben or Master Ben, but just Sir or Master is okay, too."

He pauses. "Is that clear?"

"Yes! Yes, Sir!" I say quickly and I feel the tug inside me. It's funny, I had almost forgotten "the tug"while I was with Dylan, but often when a Dom gives me some kind of direction, I feel an actual pull inside me. When I feel that pull, I pretty much do what they tell me. I had been feeling it from this man, from Sir Ben, since I got here.

He nods.

"Good girl," he says, and the way he says it, I know that I'll want to hear that from him over and over. "Here, sit back in your chair, up off the floor. If you decide to stay, you'll spend plenty of time on your knees."

I am flooded with desire, and a little noise, mphf, the sound of longing I think, escapes me.

He puts his hand on my face gently, slides his thumb into my mouth.

"Show me," he says.

I begin to serve him with my mouth, alternately licking his thumb and sucking, gently, then more firmly. I watch his face, trying to read what is pleasing to him. I know I've succeeded when he closes his eyes with a little sigh. He pulls his thumb away then, and pats my face.

Now I sigh, feeling bereft. I hope he has been pleased, there was no "good girl" from him, in fact, he tells me to sit back down. A bit reluctantly, I sit in the same chair I was in earlier, still wrapped in the afghan.

"Tell me," he says, "Why you wanted to come here."

I am embarrassed. Avoiding his eyes, I say, "I don't know... I just... sometimes I wanted to do more stuff than Dylan did, and he didn't want to and..."

I paused, just remembering how awful that felt, the longing to give and to serve.

Master Ben interrupts the memory.

"I want to hear that part, little one, the part you don't want to tell me. Tell me."

"Yes, Sir," I say, with just a touch of reluctance. "I... it's hard to explain. Sometimes I just had this feeling... It was so strong. I just wanted to really give myself to him. Well..."

I paused thinking about that. "I don't know if it was him I wanted to give myself to, really. But I wanted to give myself to... to someone who wanted to..."

My voice almost trailed off, but I managed to add, "give myself to someone who wanted to take me. Who would want me to obey them and please them. Someone who would..." whispering now, "discipline me. You know, Sir, like punish me when needed."

Then, I dared to glance up at him, and he had such a pleased look on his face that I wasn't afraid for at least a minute.

"Are you ashamed of wanting that?" He asked.

"I... Yes. Yes, Sir, I guess I am."

"That's ok," he says. "We will spank the shame out of you."

He laughs. I laugh, too, just a little bit.

"There's no shame in wanting to serve," he says. "You don't know yet if you're a submissive or a slave, and we don't know what service you can best offer. But training school will help you discern that."

"Sir," I say. "Master Ben, I do want to stay. I don't want to leave. Please."

"Then you should stay."

THEMES: breasts, dominance/submission, menage-a-trois, f/f,
mother/stepdaughter, oral sex, workplace fantasy

The Beard

By Ralph Greco Jr.

I've come to see myself somewhat like the stereotypical bartender — with my buffers, files and paints, I hear all manner of confessions across the pitted, paint-splattered expanse of my little manicuring table. I know as much about some of my ladies' personal lives as any family physician or priest. To many my Mediterranean heritage — the olive skin and dark eyes that are the result of it — give me an air of exotic distinction in the insular, affluent East Coast town where I have had my tidy, ten-chaired shop for the past decade.

Listening intently, I just keep right on cleaning, filing and 'touching up,' and I did just that with Marguerite.

The tall, strawberry-blonde treated herself to my shop once a week, keeping her long, red nails in pristine shape, her hair consistently attended. Her figure — athletic, legs long and trim, bust small but firm, medium and high — the woman looked closer to my thirty-nine years then her actual age, which she hinted was nearer fifty. She was exactly my five-foot seven height and always impeccably dressed in thin cut, long skirts and matching bolero jackets, speaking in a slight French accent that would tickle me just about perfectly as I worked on her strong hands. And although I never dare hope a woman I might be attracted to is gay, I did sense Marguerite flirting with me ever so slightly.

On her next appointment, my doubt went out the window.

"This is my stepdaughter, Michele," Marguerite said, introducing the young girl who had walked into the shop with her.

Although they shared no blood, the younger woman was the near spitting image of Marguerite, just thirty-some years younger. Same tiny blue eyes, same light cream complexion and same strong, thin body, just firmer and tighter on the twenty-something.

"She doesn't speak much English," Marguerite continued. "But we'll make do."

And surprisingly, we did. The two women spoke French and then Marguerite translated (my high-school French was way too rusty for their repartee). Through the conversation, I found Michele staring at me as deeply as Marguerite had. Could I handle this 'double-duty' attention?

"She is very beautiful, yes?" Marguerite asked, just as I finished Michele's nails.

"Very," I answered and Marguerite translated to the younger woman who coyly smiled, then whispered to her mother in French.

"Ah, yes," Marguerite said. "We need some help with waxing."

I stood as did they. The thought of getting Michele in a compromising position, at the very least alone (I had no idea what 'kind of' waxing she needed) tore at my professional veneer. I would have given almost anything to see this wonderful young creature naked, to be that close to her light skin, to delicately touch her, all desires I had for her stepmother.

The shop was busy so nobody really noticed the three of us walking to the three small waxing rooms at the back of the salon.

"Michele finds you as attractive as I do," Marguerite whispered as we entered the tiny pink room.

Marguerite took the only chair as her stepdaughter hopped up on the table. I wasn't about to disturb so perfect a scenario with rules, besides, I rationalized, didn't Marguerite have to translate? I went over to the rolling metal supply table and out of the corner of my eye caught Michele removing her sweater.

Just what kind of waxing were we getting into here?

"I'm not..." I tried, turning back to the young girl.

Michele was out of her bra in a flash, sitting there topless, smiling at me.

"If you please," Marguerite said, from behind me.

As dumb as I can be sometimes, I finally realized we were not in this room for a waxing. I simply walked across the room and kissed Michele deep on her thick red lips. Hell, I thought, I could be led as easily as anybody, especially to something I really wanted to do.

"No, no. Kiss her breasts," I heard Marguerite say, and as I leaned to do so I heard the unmistakable sound of Marguerite unzipping her skirt. Through slightly puckered lips, I gently sucked on Michele's quickly rising brown nipples, stretching her the pale skin of her perfectly pert, B-cups just enough to make her solid small breasts bounce. A 'mother-daughter' scenario wasn't one I had ever indulged in but if these ladies were ok with it, who was I to complain?

"Remove your smock," Marguerite softly ordered.

I straightened and complied. She then spoke a few words in French and Michele reached up and under my shirt with both hands to cup my heavy breasts. A few more words were spoken between the two as Michele deftly opened the buttons on my work shirt, helped me discard it and then sat back smiling as I let my bra fall.

"Take down your jeans," Marguerite said and I stepped back from Michele, unsnapped my pants and slowly slid them down my long legs. I stepped out of them and stood before Michele (in front of me) and Marguerite (behind me) in just my pink thong.

"You have a wonderfully tight bottom," Marguerite said matter-of-factly.

Her long nails which I had just worked so diligently to perfect now stroked my ass. I turned to look over my shoulder.

"No, no," she said. "Keep your eyes on Michele."

I did as asked, catching the slightest glimpse of the older woman's long tan legs, widely spread across the metal chair where she sat. Aware that, so far, Marguerite had ordered or facilitated every action, I was infatuated with her accented confident domme-ness, how she just simply assumed I'd obey.

Another few words of French were exchanged and then Michele knelt in front of me, peeling my undies off me with one fluid movement.

"Close your eyes and turn around," Marguerite said. I did so.

Sure, I was the boss, none of the ladies who worked for me would ever dare traipse back to an obviously occupied waxing room, let alone where they could, by now, quickly assume I had stepped to with a client. My shop isn't that big after all. Still, it was so hot, having to stand sandwiched between these two, detection not more than a closed accordion door away. What was happening was surely the kinkiest activity I had ever engaged in, and in my near four decades on the planet I had engaged in a few.

Yet another French phrase and then Michele scooted forward from her crouch on the cool, tile floor and placed her mouth deep into my already flooding sex.

"From the moment I saw you I wanted you," Marguerite whispered as her daughter softly attacked my wet lips.

"Your good nature, your attention, your professionalism," she listed as Michele traced her hands up my legs.

I felt myself rocking up on my toes, swooning.

"You watch, you allow," Marguerite continued, her words coming slower now, her breathing quicker.

God, my pussy was heavy. Michele was deep up in me, tickling my lips with the slight licks, her little flickering tongue teasing my clit to ache.

"Your strength is astounding," Marguerite said and I heard her gasp as Michele traced her hands across to knead my ass.

I was pulled tight into the young girl's face as I felt her tongue pressed across my clitoris and then inch down my velvet opening.

"You... are... quite... a... woman, Toni," Marguerite quietly added.

Michele was grabbing my cheeks hard. I saw her perfect shoulders, muscled and tight, from her strained position. Aching to turn, I somehow kept facing forward, reveling in how Marguerite wanted me positioned and how terrible the tease was that I couldn't see her. I didn't even want to consider the past naughty trouble these two might have gotten into, together like this and all on their own.

"I want to see you like this always," I heard Marguerite say from someplace.

Her voice was far off and breathy, deep and thick like the wetness between my legs. Michele teased my opening with her strong tongue as I tried to pull free from the torture but only managed to stay where I was with her strong hands clutching my butt. Finally, finally, after what I knew was only seconds but seemed to have been hours, the young girl pushed her tongue deep into my pussy and pushed her face into my thick triangle of dark hair. I bucked forward as I felt that quick rise that only occurs when I'm as turned on as I was right then. I clenched my ass, Michele lapped at my clit and Marguerite cried out.

I came so hard I nearly lost my balance.

Having your own shop has advantages... and headaches. There are the late hours. There is the constant worry to make payroll, cover expenses, all thoughts of survival down on your head all the time. There is the constant swallowing of pride agreeing with customers even when you know she might be wrong. For the head-strong woman I can be, rising above in all ways can be difficult, but I had learned that I could never really work for another person and survive, so I had to make my business work. If that meant quelling the hot temper my father had been so famous for, and had unfortunately passed to his only daughter, then so be it.

The old man had taught me the self-reliance and the strength Marguerite found so attractive. But there were plenty of women (and men for that matter) who didn't find my no-nonsense approach fun to be around. I had few friends and dated infrequently... not that there was a large lesbian community in my town.

Marguerite's easy-going yet confident/dominant stance in our first 'meeting' — her calm suggestion of positions and actions, the way she just assumed everything would flow — eased the usual pressures off my shoulders. To be able to lose myself in a situation where I could be the submissive, the willing, sit-back-and-enjoy-it-all victim had been one of the most thrilling sexual experiences of my life.

When the front door opened at five-thirty, I literally felt Michele and Marguerite's energy enter my small shop. As I mentioned, there are some advantages to owning your own business. I had scheduled Marguerite and her stepdaughter well past closing time.

"Hello," Marguerite said as Michele simply beamed at me.

Both women wore tight pastel-colored skirts with matching jackets over light silk blouses. If not for the two tight lines to the side of Marguerite's right eye the two could have easily been mistaken for sisters.

"You both look perfect," I said as they sat down.

The late afternoon sunlight broke through my half-drawn blinds, setting both women's hair ablaze.

"Like twins?" Marguerite asked.

"Like twins," I agreed.

"Close the shop," she said.

"Of course," I said and rose to attend to our privacy by throwing down the blinds and locking the front door. As it occurred to me that I was no longer in control, again, the wetness between my legs increased. Marguerite had made a simple soft suggestion and I had sprung into action.

Was I already under her spell?

"I was thinking about you two all week," I said walking back to the pair

"And we you," Marguerite said. "Michele and I have yet to find a woman with your qualities."

"Do you often share lovers?" I asked, sitting across from them at the front nail station

"In Paris we did, sometimes," Marguerite started. "When Michele's father died, we were quite the talk of the town."

"No doubt."

"But I bored of France and Michele so wanted to see America."

The two suddenly stood, Michele cut to my right and Marguerite to my left.

"Toni," Marguerite said, giving me her hand as I stood and came from my station. She walked me, with Michele to our side, dead center of my quiet salon.

"Close your eyes," she said and I did so.

"Now we are going to move around you."

My legs started to quiver with the idea of these two stunning women circling me.

"Reach out, but don't touch high," Marguerite instructed. "Avoid our faces. I do not want you to know whom you touch."

I suddenly understood why they were dressed the same.

"But first..." Marguerite continued and I felt kisses, two to each cheek in that stereotypical French style. "Strip."

Keeping my eyes closed, I was out of my sweatshirt and jeans in seconds. I hadn't worn any underwear in hopeful anticipation of just such a moment.

I was naked save for my socks in seconds.

"Now reach out," Marguerite said. "Touch us."

And I did. The two women circled me. I was kissed on the lips, bitten lightly on the ear. Big hands I knew to be Marguerite's cupped my breasts while a tight mouth I knew to be Michele's kissed down my belly and into my pubic hair. All the time I reached out, folding open a jacket here, or stroking a tight thigh there. I'd be convinced I had Marguerite in my grasp, her slightly larger breasts pulling tightly against my grasping hand, but then the women's hand met mine and I knew it had to be Michele.

The game was as intense as it was erotic. I was once again on display for them, aching to open my eyes, but stopped, because I knew it was not yet permitted, if it ever would be. I felt myself swooning to their kisses, flooding terribly, about to cry out, when the circle suddenly stopped. I sensed one of the women leave the immediate area. I almost opened my eyes then, but was suddenly wrapped in a strong hug.

"You are so very beautiful," Marguerite said as I nearly fell, realizing it was she who now held me.

"As are you," I said, opening my eyes finally.

"I am afraid you will not think so if you see me naked."

"I doubt that, Marguerite," I said.

She took me from her embrace and quickly said something to her daughter behind her.

Michele walked behind her stepmother and slowly peeled the older women's jacket from her shoulders. Marguerite stared at me the entire time Michele undressed her. The perfect long figure of Marguerite emerged from the silk and cotton folds. When she had her mother stripped to a light blue teddy, Michele cheated back and Marguerite stepped forward, lifting one three-inch heel then the other as she kicked her fallen clothes to the side.

"The rest is for you to remove… if you wish," she offered.

Christ, could this woman get any more attractive. Her hesitation made her seem even more resolute and strong.

I placed a hand on each of her shoulders.

"I very much wish," I said, kissing Marguerite's lips, then her chin, then her freckled throat as I ran my hands across the teddy's straps, letting them fall.

I followed the material's descent with my mouth, stopping briefly to kiss each of Marguerite's little round breasts as they were bared. The teddy stopped at her waist and I pulled it down with my teeth as I knelt to the older woman's belly and then down to her light brown patch of pubic hair. I was about to take the teddy off but Michele knelt from behind her stepmother leaving me the pleasure of burying my face in Marguerite's sex while she took off the teddy.

It took me no time at all to get Marguerite moaning. She ran her long nails (the nails I had so often worked on) through my thick hair. She spoke French as I kissed my way into her tight rindy sex and to her knotty clitoris. When I felt her begin a slow ride, I pulled back and looked up, over her tight belly, to her hands pulling her big breasts. Marguerite looked down with a look of opened-face inquisitiveness.

"You are ravishing," I said.

I smiled at her and again dove into her.

I licked and nibbled until she was groaning, she smelled so perfect and sweet, so open wet and tight. I knew I could get Marguerite off quickly... not so much from my skill but from how wet she was and how easily she had let go sitting behind me and her daughter last week.

"Please..." she sighed.

Whether this was a plea for me to stop or continue, I didn't much care. I found Marguerite's engorged thick clit and sucked on it as tightly as I could.

I knew Michele was there, I knew I was kneeling on the cold floor of my shop, I knew right outside shoppers walked unaware of me eating Marguerite in the middle of my nail-salon, but all I cared about right then was feeling Marguerite rocking over me. When I finally managed my hands to her waist, she began to shudder and I assumed came as I pulled her into me.

"Na...na...ah. Ah!" Marguerite screamed as I pushed my tongue to the center of her clit.

"Ah, ah... Toni. Toni!"

I licked Marguerite a few seconds longer to get the very last remnants of her wave. She bucked over me and moaned, leaned forward and I finished lapping at her. I leaned back on my naked haunches after a minute. Yes, it was me making her come, me, who she had lightly ordered about now two times, who had taken the lead, at least for a few seconds, getting her off in that unique way one woman can manage for another. Draping her long arms over her body, I quickly reached up and separated them.

"No," I lightly admonished. "I want to look at you."

Emboldened by her orgasm, I was leading... at least for these passing few seconds. Secretly I was aching for Marguerite to take charge again, maybe forever.

"You really like what you see?" she asked.

"Very, very much."

Marguerite's body was very much as I had fantasized it to be. Elongated muscle that on anyone else might have begged awkwardness, but it was thin and tight on her. Her breasts were plump, perfectly rounded, light colored, with tiny nipples very much like her Michele's (again, there was no DNA between them, but they did resemble one another almost to a disconcerting degree). Her belly was tight without being unnaturally muscled, there was a beauty mark to the right of her belly button and her long legs were flared evenly to present that trim brown mound of pubic hair that had smelled so sweet.

I must have sat staring for a good three minutes when Marguerite looked over her shoulder and spoke to Michele. The younger girl came from around the older, squatted to kiss me on the cheek, smiled and then struggled to whisper in my ear:

"You make her very 'appy," she managed in one quick breath and then stood and left the shop.

I stood as Marguerite turned to gather her clothes and yet again another flash went off in my brain. Michele had been her mother's 'beard.'

"You didn't need to do that," I said to Marguerite's slightly freckled back. "I wanted you so much as it was."

"As did I you," she said, turning to me. "But how could I be sure?"

"Are you sure now?"

"Yes," she said.

Again, she was revealing a deep vulnerability that informed her confidence in a way that aroused me. I did not completely understand the dichotomy and what it was doing to my libido, but I smiled and motioned to the two chairs to our right. We sat and Marguerite spoke as she dressed.

"My stepdaughter is young, impetuous. But I assure you she wanted you as well."

"I gathered and I am flattered."

"But she is not like me," Marguerite said, taking my hand. "After my marriage ended I knew I could no longer deny my les–"

"Yes," I interrupted, knowing of what she spoke, desires not answered for a long time, deep heartfelt aches, and longings.

I had felt such a pull to Marguerite, a kinship, from the first time I had met her to that very moment. Michele, on the other hand, while intoxicatingly attractive and resourceful, I knew was simply sowing as many wild oats as possible, with whatever gender, with or without her stepmom's participation. And while I was greatly attracted to the younger girl, I was completely smitten by her mother.

"It has been so long for me," Marguerite continued. "So long to find a woman I desire to be with."

"Me, too," I said as I reached across and kissed her lips.

* * * * *

It's been four months.

I have seen Michele often and while I am still wildly attracted to her effervescence and still harbor deep fantasies about her firm little breasts and quick strong tongue, I would never jeopardize the relationship that her stepmother and I have been building. I still marvel at the chance Marguerite took 'introducing' herself via her daughter.

The possibility that I may have fallen for the younger of the two women was a risk she took for the slight chance (or so she thought) to get closer to me. Of course, I coddle the notion that Marguerite is intuitive enough to have known I wanted her from the moment we set eyes on each other and the seduction with her daughter was all part of her plan.

I so desperately need and want Marguerite that I sit on the edge of my seat at work just waiting for her to appear for her almost daily appointments.

And the tips are just as generous as always.

THEMES: cross dressing, domestic submission, dominance/submission, exhibitionism, masturbation, oral sex, sissy play

Alice

By M.Christian

It started with the laundry — how ironic is that?

Laundry was a kind of blind spot for Al. Ask him to take out the garbage, drive five hundred miles to help out a friend, weed the back yard or cook (he made a mean-ass clam chowder he was particularly proud of) and it would get done so quickly and so neatly that jaws would drop and eyes would pop. No muss, no fuss: just a well-executed chore or perfectly performed task.

But ask him to do the laundry, and by the grudging production he made of the whole thing — stripping the bed, picking up crumpled piles of clothing, hauling baskets downstairs, stuffing the washer — you'd think he'd been asked to give Karl Malden a sponge bath.

At first, Jeannine hadn't been bothered by this quirk.

"Just the usual breaking-in stuff," she'd thought to herself and told friends who asked about the couple's experiment in living together. "Nothing to worry a war-crimes tribunal about."

* * * * *

Four months later, she'd begun to think, "Okay, this is starting to really bug me," and clench her smooth hands into tight, white fists.

Six months in, she was debating with herself how best to dispose of his body.

She had to be honest with herself and admit that he tried. But somehow, his trying only made it worse. Huffing and puffing like a kid asked to eat his broccoli, he'd make such a big deal out of doing laundry that Jeannine didn't know whether to make him stand in a corner or give him a Golden Globe for acting. Even when Al seemed to want to do the laundry, earnestly "helping out around the house" on her birthday, or when he'd done something spectacularly dumb and needed to do some housework Hail Marys, it didn't work out. Her favorite red dress, white shift, the linen, even a suede jacket went in — and what came out went straight to Goodwill.

Despite Al's laundry issues, he and Jeannine had it pretty good: Al's underground comic, The Snitch, was doing remarkably well — well enough that he didn't need a real job yet. Jeannine's store, Deco Mojo, was paying for their rent and a little more. Unlike a lot of their friends, they'd been together a little over a year with no sign of impending breakup or nasty drama.

In all their time together, including the months before cohabitation and after making the big leap into it, Jeannine and Al had a pretty cooperative relationship: some gives, some takes, fair play all the way around. Al did the shopping this week, Jeannine the next. This month Al paid the phone bill, next month Jeannine did. Except for the issue of the laundry, they kept everything fair and even between them.

That's not quite true, though. Everything was fair and even except for the law when it came to laundry and one other situation: the bedroom.

* * * * *

But that's also not quite true — mainly because for Al and Jeannine, the bedroom was only one of the places where you fucked around. The Outdoors, you see, did it for Jeannine. The more out the better, especially when there was a real risk they'd get spotted by someone — extra-especially when they could be spotted by more than just one someone. Parking garages, baseball games, movie theaters, hiking trails — they'd tried them all.

Al called it "eye-porn." The way Jeannine reacted to being watched was like the way guys reacted to looking at anything and anyone sexy. He loved it almost as much as Jeannine did: crawling up the fire escape to the roof, giggling and whispering like schoolkids, laying out a blanket on gravel still warm from sunlight, a kiss, more kisses, clothes off, hands roaming, cock very hard, pussy very wet, fucking long and slow, then hard and fast knowing that someone could be looking at them any second or that hundreds — maybe thousands — were doing just that already.

But what did Al like? She didn't know.

"I'm not complaining, mind you," she said to some of her friends when they'd she and Al had first moved in together. "Not at all."

Four months later, "I just can't figure him out" was the order of the day.

At six months, she was wondering what terrible secret he was hiding, what skeletons he had in his closet.

Then, one lazy Saturday afternoon — chores completed, laundry carefully ignored — they curled up together on their plush, painfully bright orange sofa and flipped through mail, stopping in the middle of bills and miscellaneous flyers to glance at the Victoria's Secret catalog..

"Wow," Al said, brown eyes wide as Jeannine flipped through the glossy pages. "Pretty."

The times they'd gone to the museum and snuck in a quick blow-job amongst the French Impressionists, all Al had said was, "Nice." When they went to friends' gallery openings and fucked ferociously in the grimy bathrooms, all Al said was, "Eh." "Good" was what Al called his world-renowned chowder, and how he described their sex life.

In all their months together, Jeannine had never heard Al call anything else by that one word of praise. Until, that is, page seventy-nine of the Victoria Secret catalog.

That night, Jeannine smiled to herself. It was time, she thought, for Al's skeleton to come out of the closet. Time, with the dreaded laundry, for him to come out — and play.

* * * * *

"Perfect. Absolutely perfect. Or else," Jeannine said, uncomfortable with even the idea of a threat — but obviously excited by it.

"Or else?" Al said, as uncomfortable as she was with the threat — and just as excited.

"Or else you're going to be very intimate with some of my more intimates, Al. Do you get me?"

Al was speechless. But his face said what his voice couldn't.

"Good. Now, let's get it all done right, Al: fabric softener, the right temperature, no mixed colors, no running, nothing wrong. Perfect. No mistakes, Al." She cast him a cool glance. "I'm going out for a few hours, got some store stuff to take care of, and when I get back, I expect the laundry to be done like it's never been done before."

Then she went out, with a wide, wicked smile on her lips.

* * * * *

"Let me see," she said, four hours and some-odd minutes later. "Show me what you've got."

"Ah, sure," Al said, nerves making him hesitate. He stammered. "Sure thing, babe."

"Don't call me 'babe.' Not yet, at any rate. Now show me. And this had better be good."

"Yes…" he said, and started to address her as something that began with 'b' but caught himself, substituting a quick "'b' right back" and a smile.

The first basket was full to overflowing with sheets, pillow cases, blankets, and towels. Jeannine tried to keep the smile off her face as he pulled out each neatly folded bundle. Creases almost made her giggle with joy, seams made her flash some pearly white teeth — but she fought to keep her face stony and firm.

"Now the next one," she said.

The next basket was packed with slacks, jeans, blouses, socks, boxers, bras, shirts, and panties. Al may have screwed up every other attempt at laundry, but this time he gleamed, shown, sparkled, was absolutely spotless: she may have barely kept the smile from her face before, but now it took every ounce of control for her to keep from laughing and giving him a big hug — and the laundry had nothing to do with it.

She had to find something wrong, though. That was the game, after all. "What's this?" she said, holding up a pair of panties.

"Um, er… It's your … panties."

"That's right, it's my favorite pair: soft, pearlescent, pure white with the frilly waistband and the tiny blue flower right in the middle. Right there. See the flower? But there's something about this flower, Al, something very, very bad."

Al swallowed hard but didn't say anything.

"You see, Al, my favorite pair of silky panties has four little green leaves next to that sweet little flower. Four. Not two, not three, not five — four. Now, Al, I want you to take these and tell me how many little green leaves there are next to that so-sweet little flower."

Al took the panties in suddenly moist hands, turned them carefully until the little flower faced him. Just as Jeannine had never heard Al use the word "pretty" before, not at the museum, not in a gallery. She'd never really seen him hold something reverently before.

"Three," Al said, glancing up from the panties to look her in the face. His eyes were wide and gently moist.

"That's right, Al. Three. Not four, three. One of my flowers is missing. That's not a good thing. Not a good thing at all. I asked you to do something and you didn't do it. I'm afraid, Al, that you'll have to be punished."

Al's face lit with a soft smile.

"I understand."

He seemed to want to add something else (Ma'am, Sir, Mistress, something like that) but didn't know what to say, yet.

"Good. Now strip."

Al's smile grew, took on a sweetness and a subtle 'thank you,' and he did as he was told.

Next to one of the baskets went his hurriedly unfolded shirt, shoes, pants, socks, and underwear, until he stood in front of her, tall and lean, all long bones and tight muscles, and very, very hard.

Jeannine looked at his gently bobbing cock. It took a lot of control not to reach out and stroke it, suck it.

"Very good," she said, her voice catching in her throat. She doubted she'd ever seen him as hard.

"Very, very good. Now, Al..." she tossed him the sheer panties "...put these on."

At first Al didn't do anything. He just stood in front of her, very hard, with a strange expression on his face. Later, when she had time to really think about it, Jeannine would realize that among the emotions that were zapping around inside her boy-friend's mind — desire, suspicion, shame, fear, to name a few — the one that finally won out, that made him reach down and put o ne foot, then the other, into the satin undies and slowly, sensually draw them up his body, was relief.

"Very nice," Jeannine said, surprising herself at her own sincerity.

He really did look ... not pretty, but definitely very sexy: his very hard cock tented the white material like he was trying

to shoplift a javelin, and the sheer material was already growing damp at the end with pearly pre-come. Again, it took all of
Jeannine's control not to just lick the end, taste the salty bitterness.

"Very sexy, Al. No, that's not right. You're not really Al, are
you? Not right now."

Al hung his head slightly, pulled his elbows and knees in,
shrinking, getting younger, the rough and tumble Al fading away
as Jeannine watched.

"Alice?" Jeannine said, the inspiration like a small shock.
"Your name is Alice. Isn't that right ... Alice?"

Al, her boyfriend, was gone. Alice, her girlfriend with the
white satin panties, very big clit, and very small boobs, nodded
slowly, happily.

"You're very pretty, Alice, in nothing but your white panties.
Very sexy. Do you feel sexy, Alice?"

Alice smiled radiantly, saying wordlessly: Yes, very much so.

"Turn around, Alice. Show me your sexy little body. Show me
what you've got, slut."

Alice chewed a thumbnail, eyes wide and moist.

"Do it, Alice! Or do you want me to be upset?"

Jeannine wanted to laugh, to cry, at how excited they both
seemed to feel. It wasn't a game she'd played before — and never
would have thought about playing with Al — but with Alice it
seemed right, natural, and most of all, way too much fun.

Alice's eyes grew even wider. Then, slowly, shyly, she turned
around, giving Jeannine a hesitant view of her boyish body.

"Very sexy," Jeannine said, suddenly aware of her own wetness. "I really like you in my panties. In fact, I think you look even
better in my panties than I do. They're yours now."

"T-thank you," Alice said. Even her voice was soft and almost
innocent.

Jeannine leaned forward and grabbed hold of Alice's huge clit
in a powerful grip. Alice was startled, but Jeannine hung on and
wouldn't let her pull away. "You forget your place, Alice. Do you
want me to be displeased?"

"N-no," stammered Alice, hands falling to Jeannine's.
Touching, but not trying to pull them away.

"'No,' what? Who am I, Alice? What do you call me?"

Alice's face burned bright red. Her lips quivered but no words
came out.

"Say it, Alice — or I put you to bed without any supper."

"Mistress..." whispered Alice. Then, with a bit more force: "Yes, Mistress."

It was like a weight had been lifted.

"That's right. I'm your Mistress. Don't you forget it, either."

She let go of Alice's clit. The thin girl took a half step back in response.

"No, no, Mistress, I won't forget," Alice said, composing herself.

"You'd better not," Jeannine reached out and ran her fingers up the length of Alice's very hard, rhythmically flexing clit.

"So beautiful..." she said, almost a whisper.

Shaking her head slowly, as if to clear it, she said in a louder voice, "Now then, slut. Where were we? Oh, yes, that's right. You were giving me a show. I like a good show."

Jeannine leaned back as if to inspect her new plaything.

"Why don't you show me how hard that clit of yours really is. Rub it for me, stroke it through your new panties. Do it. Do it now."

"Yes, Mistress," Alice said, her voice honey and all manner of sweetness. Palm down, she dropped one hand down to the front of her panties and slowly started to rub herself.

"That's it," Jeannine said, gently parting her own legs in response, as if Alice's clit was somehow connected directly to her own. "That's it."

"Thank you, Mistress," Alice said, her eyes glazing over in pleasure.

As she rubbed, stroked herself, the front of her panties got wetter and wetter. Soon, the pale material was almost transparent, giving Jeannine a perfect view of the thin girl's monstrous clit.

"Thank you..." said Alice.

"Oh, yes, you slut. You love this, don't you, slut? You love it, being the nasty little girl, putting on a show just for me. Yeah, that's it; rub it, rub that sweet clit for me. Make those panties nice and hot and wet and sticky. Stroke it for me, stroke it..."

Alice bit down on her lip, her breath coming in shorter and shorter hisses until, finally, she didn't make any sound at all but her body tensed as if a kind of wonderful voltage slammed through her. She went rigid, locked tight in a shuddering orgasm, the front of her panties suddenly soaked with her sticky juices.

In a barely controlled fall, Alice dropped first to her knees and then face first onto the carpet. She lay there for a long time, her body quivering and quaking with release, breaths now heavy and slow.

"Very, very good, slut," Jeannine said, reaching up under her simple skirt to hook a thumb into the waistband of her own, every-day panties. "That was quite a show. Quite a nice show. I'm very impressed."

The panties came off, soaked through. She tossed them aside.

"In fact, come here, Alice," she said, her voice a husky whisper, "and taste how impressed I am."

Slowly, weak only in body, Alice got to her knees and moved over to Jeannine until her face was parallel with Jeannine's downy pubic hairs. Now it was Jeannine's turn to really smile, as the game got even better for her. Leaning down, she parted her plush lips, giving Alice a view of her very wet folds and pulsing clit.

"Taste," she managed to get out before her voice completely caught in her throat.

Alice did. Alice did, indeed. Nuzzling up between Jeannine's strong thighs, she flicked her tongue over Jeannine's clit. Hard and fast, slow and soft, Alice licked. Standing above her, but at that instant miles away, Jeannine moaned and bucked, dipped and swayed, in response.

Finally, the pressure Alice was applying peaked and Jeannine cried — her version short and sharp and loud compared to Alice's near-silent and long — and she slid down, landing hard on the floor at Alice's feet.

Her body still working, she threw her hands around Alice, her girlfriend, and Al, her boyfriend, and cried hot tears of pleasure and wonderful discovery.

* * * *

Some stories really do have happy endings. Al's comic work continued to do well, receiving both critical acclaim and financial success. Jeannine's store became a hallmark of the neighborhood. Al and Jeannine, and Alice and Jeannine were very happy together — and their whites were whiter, their colors brighter, than ever before.

I Like You On Me.

By Aravielle

I'm not going anywhere. I have no interest in going anywhere, at least until it hurts too much or I just can't take it or you say, "see ya."

I'd rather have you part time sometimes than not at all. You are absolutely not what I was looking for but you are absolutely what I needed.

I don't think you understand the enormity of that statement. I suspect if you knocked on my door in 10 years, I wouldn't bat an eye. I would just grab your hand and go wherever.

I'm lying here wondering how in a sum total of six hours or so spent with you you were able to leave such a constant ache on my body. I can close my eyes and feel you. Everywhere.

I'm expecting that it will start to fade which makes me a bit sad. I like you on me. I mean I also love you in me...

I am always extremely excited to see you, if it happens to happen, when it happens to happen.

I sent up a little wish that you sleep and get to rest your mind tonight. Completely. You can't be everything to everyone and not take care of You!

Pssssstt......

Hey you. Sir?? Could you please ever so kindly step out of my head. Pretty please. I just spent three minutes looking for my phone because of you. It was in my back pocket. SHENANIGANS!!

You don't have to apologize for handling your life. It's one of the things I find so sexy about you. You just do what you need to do. I just wish there was a little less handling of life and a little more handling of me.

Two Days Later

It has only been a few days since you were last inside me, but the physical effect has started to fade. It never really fades from my mind. I wonder if it ever will. It eventually fades from my body.

It's like a warm burning heat on my skin, inside and out. I'm always struck by how vividly I can remember your touch. It starts as a tingle in my belly and spreads across my chest like slow warmth grazing my nipples and turns into an uncomfortably warm ache that moves lower. That ache spreads across my belly, down my thighs until it culminates in between my legs as fire and damp desire for you. That full consumption of my physical and mental being takes over and pushes away all other feelings and sensations.

Even when you haven't touched me...

You said you're coming to see me and I immediately feel hungry for you. The anticipation is almost reckless. You have warned me that you are tired and recent days have been long, frustrating. I've spent hours waiting, wondering, wanting.

When you arrive, you cross the room to sit and eat the food you have brought with you. It's clear you have more than one physical need to be quenched this morning.

I slide off the chair and move to where you're sitting. I'm wearing nothing but a thin, old nightshirt. I was waiting for you. You're not even enjoying your food, just fulfilling your body's needs.

I wonder momentarily if I will serve to be the same. Will I sate your hunger? These meetings do satisfy me for a time, and then I'm ravenous all over again as soon as you leave.

I slide my arms down your shoulders as my tongue plays a tune on your neck. I make small sounds in your ear, but I do not want to disturb you. As my hand reaches to your waist, you grab it gently and give me a look that stings.

You are annoyed at my impatience. I am never satisfied and today has tested your limits. I just wanted to feel you, not stop you. I flinch slightly and pull away.

I walk to lay on the bed quietly, my face turned away. I start to play music, low and quiet in the background. I want to drown out my head. I want the rebuke to fade. I know I am not the source of your annoyance, at least I hope.

I hear you finish your meal and start to shower. Maybe that will rinse away what has caused all of this tension in you.

When you are finished you move to the bed slowly. I am laying face down. The sting is gone, but so is my ache for you. It's not gone, but it is subdued.

You haven't said a word. Your hand starts on my lower back and moves ever so slowly down across my skin. Your touch is searching, as if you are feeling something you've discovered for the first time.

Contemplating, your hand moves between my legs and I am wet, very wet. I've been waiting for you for so long. You push my legs apart firmly and before I know, your fingers are inside me, deep, again searching.

You know my body too well and it reacts to your touch.

I don't want to want you.

I feel the sting of your hand across my flesh and wonder how painful it will become. Will there be more? I hope so. You slide your fingers inside me hard and I start to cum immediately. You stop before I finish and you hear me whimper.

Your fingers pry my lips apart so I taste myself on you as you order me to turn over, lay my head off the edge of the bed and open my mouth. My body is laid out for you to see. You place your hand on the back of my neck and grab into my hair to position me just so.

You start to fuck my mouth, deep and slow, all the way into my throat. You let up enough for me to breathe but you are relentless in your movements. You know that makes me so hot.

I reach my hand down toward my clit and you pin my arm to the bed.

I hear you growl. "No."

At the same time, I feel you explode down my throat. I lay there, eyes closed, licking my lips but I'm still unsatisfied. My body is slowly writhing against the sheets. I just want you to fuck me!

I don't move away when you slide your fingers inside me and then slide one into my ass as your tongue finds my clit. I grind myself into your mouth as you feel me grip you tighter and I cry out.

Finally! You took so long!

I beg you, barely a whisper.

"Please fuck me, now."

Two more days later.

Morning wake up routine: feel the sun through my eyelids, take a slow deep breath, stretch my naked body like a cat from my shoulders to my toes, feel my mind come to consciousness.

Before one thought enters my mind there you are, the thoughts of you are right where I don't want you to be, but where I want you to stay forever.

Every morning you're like a warm breath on my neck that moves down my shoulder and drifts across my whole body. In my mind, you make a fleeting stop at my nipples and that warm breath becomes a slow burning heat. I am so turned on.

That's how it starts, every morning since our first meeting. You don't even have to touch me to make me feel like that. Maybe that is why I wake up in the middle of the night and so early lately. I just want to feel you when I actually can't. I want you, badly. It's so real in those first few moments and if I don't open my eyes I can make it last for some time. It's the very best part of my mornings.

This is what I mean when I say I feel you on my skin, in my skin.

THEMES: cock worship, dominance/submission, impact play (flogger whip),
master/slave, punishment, woman in uniform workplace fantasy

Gertrude

By M.Christian

He doesn't look like much. Still, when I look at the picture he sent me I get a quiet rush, a reverberation of what it was like.

I didn't feel anything like that when I knocked on his door that night, four years ago. It was routine, a noise complaint. I remember thinking, as I walked up the steps to the little house on 4467 Pierce Street, that anyone who blasted Beethoven couldn't be a lot of trouble to deal with. I was wrong.

He'd opened the door on the third knock. I sized him up the instant it swung open: white Caucasian male, 35 to 37 years old, approximately 140 pounds, curly brown hair, green eyes, no facial hair or obvious distinguishing markings. He'd been wearing jeans, tennis shoes, and a faded orange sweatshirt with the brooding face of his favorite composer on the front, whose 5th Symphony was rattling the windows.

At the Academy, they teach you never to make assumptions that even the most innocent face can hide a nasty perp.

"Treat every situation as a potentially dangerous one."

If you do, you'll freak out in a matter of months. It had taken me a while, more than anything because of who I am: my size, my age, that I'm a woman — but I'd still managed to develop a set of cop instincts.

The Academy would say to watch your ass, but my guts said that he was just some innocent music fan.

As it turned out, the Academy was closer to the truth.

"Shit!" he'd said, with a comic intensity that made me smile despite myself, "Sorry, Officer."

He dropped back into the place, moving quickly towards a wall-sized stereo set-up, and Beethoven dropped down to just a percussive rumble.

"Got a little carried away I guess. You know Ludwig. Gets your blood stirred up."

I can't remember what I said. I do remember, though, what I was staring at. You see a lot of shit when you're a cop, but in quiet little Bakersfield you don't see that much.

I knew what I was looking at, of course; I'd seen more than my fair share in the magazines I kept hidden at home. Still, it was one thing to know something exists and quite another to see it personally.

I guess I must have stared for quite a while, because I was suddenly aware that he was looking at me. Shaking it off, I glanced at him and met a sly smile and those sparkling green eyes.

I didn't say a word as he closed the door behind me.

* * * * *

My ID says GERTRUDE PARROW. I still hate Momma for that, a name no one, let alone a kid, should get stuck with. To everyone except the Sergeant it's Jeri, not Gerty, and certainly not Gertrude. Usually all it takes is a frown and a low growl to get it corrected.

The Academy taught me a lot of things that weren't on the curriculum. Like female officers will always get the shit work, especially in little burgs like Bakersfield, and that we're going to get damned little respect, from citizens and especially from other cops. Momma always said I was a fast learner and that was a lesson I picked up extra quick. After my first two weeks I put aside Gertrude and built up Jeri, a tightly-wound, non-nonsense, ball-breaking bitch. Of course being a little more than six foot helps, as does carrying 160 in firm muscles. Wasn't always that way, I had to build Jeri up in more ways than just attitude.

I was strong. I was mean. No one messed with me, not even my 'fellow officers.' I was also lonely.

I attracted some men, of course, and even some women, but you could see in their eyes that they wanted Jeri and not the whole package, which was Jeri but also Gertrude.

Until that day he played Beethoven too loud — and I saw the whip.

* * * * *

I didn't ask, "Is it real?" as he got me a drink from the kitchen. I didn't need to. It had a very... lived-in look. Black leather strips, about a dozen or so strands. It looked heavy, it looked mean, it looked...

I felt myself quietly go wet staring at it.

His name was, is, Julius. You wouldn't know it to look at him, with his old sweatshirt and running shoes, but he'd been doing this kind of thing for a while. Not obvious, but definitely there when he spoke.

"So, you want to play?"

It wasn't so much a question as a mocking observation. All I could do was nod as I sipped my drink.

"Then let's," he said, smiling broadly, eyes dancing. "Or would this be assaulting a police officer?"

I smiled back, reached up and plucked my badge from my shirt. Jeri was determined; Gertrude was hungry.

He started with a kiss, not a polite peck on the cheek, but rather a forceful, hot stab with his tongue. Grabbing the back of my very short ponytail he jerked me back, hard. Gasping for air, I instead would his firm, soft lips, and strong, passionate tongue. Down deep, I felt myself respond ... on a very primal level.

"You're mine, slut," he said with a bass growl. "For the next hour you are mine, a possession, an object, a thing. You exist for one, and only one thing: to pleasure me. Do you understand me, slut?"

I agreed. I tried to make it sound like "YES, SIR!" but I'm afraid it was just little Gertrude by then, Jeri having stepped out with that first hard kiss, and instead it came out "yes... sir..."

"Now strip! Show me what you've got," he said, pulling up a battered chair and sitting, facing me.

Those men, and those few women... They'd wanted me to say those words, to growl commands, orders, but all that time I wanted to hear them, too; to put aside the badge, gun, the attitude, to put aside Jeri.

I stood, slowly because my knees were weak, and started to unbutton my shirt. I didn't intend to do it slowly, but my fingers were shaking. One button, two, three. Shirt off.

Then my boots, comically hopping braced against a door jamb — but he didn't laugh. No, he watched. Not stared, just watched, with a gleam in those green eyes like a falcon or a leopard.

I didn't know if he was going to fuck me, or consume me — and that made me all the wetter.

Naked, I stood in front of him, my juices painting my inner thighs with a sheen of want. He smiled, cruelly, and stood. He inspected me, looking at my heavy tits, my crinkled nipples, my ass, my belly, my neck, my face, into my eyes.

"You'll do," he said after a while.

"Thank you, Sir," I said in a weak voice, the carpet swaying beneath my feet.

"As an object you must meet my needs, satisfy my every desire. Do you understand me, slut?"

"Yes, Sir," I said, distinctly aware of my throbbing clit, the ache in my nipples.

Then he said it, and if I was flowing before I practically streamed after.

"Suck my cock," he said, a growl in his words, steel in his tones.

He was impressive, but I'd seen larger. But it wasn't just his cock I was begging for. He was hard, a thick length of cock just sticking out of his pants. That got me even wetter, not for the sight of it but rather the command, the order.

I got down on my knees and started to suck him like His was the only cock in the world.

Done others, probably will do many others, but His was my Master's cock, the cock I'd been ordered to suck, and so nothing could compare to it. Single-mindedly, becoming an ecstatic sucking machine, I worked on Him — his slight moans and groans a glorious kind of applause for my technique. I wanted more than anything to please him.

I guess I got a little too enthusiastic, the joy at being pushed down, at being released from my bounds as the dominant Jeri. It was a little too much for him. His small yelp was like glass shattering, as if a part of my ideal world, the world of Gertrude the sucking slave, broke, fell apart.

"Bad," he said, pulling his cock out of my mouth and sticking it back into his pants, "very bad. Obviously you're in need of some training, because a real slave, an ideal slut, would never, ever, allow her teeth to even graze the cock of her Master."

Jeri was frightened of nothing, but Gertrude, little slutty Gertrude, was terrified.

"I'm so sorry, Sir…" I pleaded in a soft little voice, bowing down towards his simple running shoes. "Please, I didn't mean to…"

I couldn't see his face, but I could hear the sneer in his voice.

"Begging is so pathetic, even for a slut. Obviously you're in need of some severe discipline."

That was it. Right then I knew what was coming next. The magazines I'd bought with their lurid fleshtones and shocking titles had prepared me some, but not enough. They'd shown me the position, on my hands and knees, head down on the old carpeting, ass high in the air, legs slightly spread to bare the lips of my cunt, but they never, and never could have, gotten me ready for the first impact of the whip.

I expected pain, but it was more than that. At first it was a gentle slap, a glancing blow across both my cheeks. That's it? I remember thinking, almost frowning into the carpet, but then there came the next blow, harder, faster, and I knew that wasn't it. Oh, no, that wasn't it at all.

The impacts came faster, a pounding rhythm that may have started on my ass but soon became a drumming tremor through my whole body. It was as if my entire being was being beaten with a regular 4x4 beat, a drum in his sensual, masterful concerto.

My ass warmed, becoming almost hot, and my cunt felt molten, melting further with each thud of the whip. Each beat was like a great wave rolling through my body, starting at my cunt and rippling through my belly, into my deep guts, thrilling my nipples and then out my mouth. At first, I thought the sound was from somewhere else. It wasn't until later that I realized that I'd groaned with each impact, an echoing deep rumble to his regular beating.

Jeri was nowhere to be found. It was just the slut, Gertrude, receiving her exquisite punishment. And it was wonderful.

He said something, and it stopped, the cessation almost as shocking as the first impact. Distantly, I was aware that he reached down and helped me up, led me like a sleepy child deeper into his apartment.

After, I looked closer at the room. I noticed the great bookshelf of dusty, and dog-headed volumes, the rack of CD's, the small pile of dirty laundry… and the brass bed. But as he led me in, I didn't see anything but his hard hand gripping my wrists, then the bed itself, vast and comforting.

"You have pleased me, slut," he said, as if from a long distance. "You have pleased me with your performance, but there's one last thing I require."

I knew what was coming next, as if a deep part of Gertrude was following some passionate script. Again, my face was down, this time in a soft comforter, arms outstretched to grip the cool metal of the brass bed. Again, my legs apart, my ass high, but this time not to receive the whip.

He entered me, cock sliding effortlessly into my hot cunt. He fucked me — and again, like with the whipping, time vanished and I became his object, his slut. I lived for his pleasure, existed to service him; it was wonderful.

We fucked that first time for what felt like hours, his strokes rocketing through me as the whip had, but this time the impacts echoed through my body, not just from my reddened ass. Slowly, he pushed me higher and higher, quickly up a slope I'd only climbed before with one of my forbidden magazines and a vibrator.

Then it happened, and shortly thereafter for him as well. The ecstasy was like a brilliant light in my eyes, a body rush, and a dreamlike collapse onto the soft comforter, onto his brass bed.

That was the first. There were many times after. Officer Jeri may have knocked on his door that first time, but it was slutty little Gertrude who returned time and time again.

Fires die, people change, eventually it faded for both of us. There have been others since, more Masters and even some Mistresses, but he'll always remain special, a first step on a long and wonderful road.

Every once and a while, I still take his photo out of my wallet and stare at his face, at those stern green eyes, and Gertrude smiles.

Laughter

By Angie Ravenstone

I met Johnny so long ago that in my mind he's always been there — a figure in the corner, lurking, maybe stalking. We had our own lives, went our own ways, and all the other cliches you want to apply. Something between us reverberated and caused a chemical reaction I didn't experience with other people.

I haven't seen him in years, this particular encounter happened three years ago, maybe more, at the height of the pandemic. At that time we talked periodically and he sensed my need for release even before I did. I don't handle stress well, so he invited me to his place to play. I knew Johnny avoided not only people but most of society. My fears about the virus were minimal, because I'd already had first wave. It hadn't killed me and logically I'd have some immunity now.

It's nice to have someone who knows, and respects, your limits. It's nice to walk into a situation with the negotiating and decision-making out of the way. Johnny knows my thresholds and my kinks, so I trust him with my holes and my safety.

Johnny had asked me to wear loose clothes, and no undergarments, probably just to make me self-conscious and aware of my body during the trip to his apartment. Feeling fabric rub in ways cloth didn't normally touch me and wondering if people were staring at my jiggling breasts spurred my body to heat in ways I had forgotten.

I blushed as I put the car into park, as my nipples stood erect to the world. That's a side effect of the multiple piercings I've had — piercings I've since removed because I found them too distracting. I would constantly find myself tugging the captive bead ring on my left nipple and spinning the two bars that formed the cross on my left.

It's a phenomenon people who don't have body piercing might not understand. The millennial in my office recently got her nose pierced and her finger perpetually resides in her nostril. When I tell her to get her finger out of her nose, she insists the jewelry is falling out and I'm too geriatric to understand. As if her generation invented a simple nose piercing.

I parked the car and headed to the building. And if you like unimportant detail, I didn't lock it. We live in a region of medium population density and if somebody wants to steal my decade old Volkswagen or the crap inside it, let them. The parking lot has a BMW, a shiny new 'raptor' pickup truck, Johnny's Toyota that's seen more of my nudity than my bedroom (I burn more at the thought) and among the other cars two Kias, which I hear are popular to steal now thanks to some hooligans on Tik-Tok.

Johnny answered the door topless and in classic navy blue sweatpants, not the fitted joggers popular these days or the yoga style or the slim walking pants with the open ankles, but good, old-fashioned, baggy, with elastic at the bottom hem that causes the fabric to bulge a bit sweatpants. Knowing Johnny, he got them from WalMart, or Dollar General, or maybe if the CEO hadn't done something to piss him off, Target. Johnny had principles. They didn't always make sense to me, but I enjoyed our conversations. Who else would treat me to orgasms, apple juice in bed, and chit chat about American imperialism?

He pulled me in, and in this well-practiced motion, he swings the door closed with one arm while curling the other around my waist and devours me with a kiss. He smells of basic men's cologne and blue Listerine. He tastes fresh and cool. His hand slips down my ass, centering my nether regions against his. The dance of our mouths and the rock in his pants draw a moan from me.

Johnny knows me better than I know myself.

I don't think we spoke a single word. No "hello" or "good to see you," we'd known each other too long for pleasantries. Within five minutes I found myself naked on his bed. Johnny retained his sweatpants as he laid on top of me, stretching my arms above my head as he restrained me by the wrists, one broad hand pinning my narrow arms.

He adeptly wound rope to make the situation more permanent, anchoring my arms somewhere beyond my view. Then, his mouth led the journey toward my other limbs as soon my ankles found themselves pulled apart and fastened "spread eagle" to allow full access to my lusty female parts.

If Johnny were a meteorologist, he would have to forecast a storm that would leave the region drenched with sporadic downpours.

And then — unexpectedly — he blindfolded me. Of all the things we'd done, this was never one of them.

"Is this okay?" he asked.

It was the first time that day he'd spoken to me, and my own voice cracked as I responded. God, I loved his gentle speech. In all these years, he'd never raised his voice to me. Even when I challenged him beyond HIS limits.

"I think so," I answered.

He stroked the exposed undersides of my arms as he kissed me. I strained to reach more of him.

"You remember what to say if it's not?" he prompted.

"May I have a glass of water?" I quickly replied, eager to get the preliminaries out of the way.

"That's right," he said.

My ears focused on the clatter of ice. Suddenly, at my side, the frigid, sweating glass rested against my ribcage. I flinched. I actually tried to recoil away from it, but Johnny's ropes wouldn't give. More clatter and then silence. Johnny kissed me again, his mouth now devoid of that inviting body temperature, the warmth replaced with sterile cold. Chilled fingers toyed with my nipple. My body vibrated with the sensation and the need — it opened something within me and I wanted deeper engagement.

But I also knew Johnny. He had a plan and if I bucked against it, he would merely withhold satisfaction all the longer. My mind drifted, wondering if maybe I would have been better off picking up a stranger for a one-night stand, because strangers don't hesitate to give dick.

Johnny toyed with his delights. Or should I say that was Johnny's sadistic pleasure? Johnny liked to push a person as close to ultimate joy as possible and deny it until the build-up to orgasm caused so much pain, the eventual release felt like reaching nirvana in the middle of an earthquake.

And I'm not talking about "Sounds like teen spirit" or "Rape me." Johnny had missed grunge, and knew nothing about my people, what it meant to be Generation X.

Suddenly, Johnny's finger plunged deep into my pussy, so far and so quickly it burned. I worried maybe I wasn't ready for such an invasion, maybe I didn't want things invading my holes. As soon as his finger withdrew, I stopped doubting, because the sucking and slickness that followed proved the initial response was surprise, not lack of desire.

I couldn't see Johnny. He made no noise. He moved no air. Something heavy and meaty, probably his palm, pushed like a foot on the brake of a car against my waxed mound as what I guessed was two fingers plunged deeply into me. This became the routine. Whatever was on top of me applied pressure as fingers explored my rippling insides, tracing the edges, pounding the walls. Was he trying to do home renovations in there?

Every time he vacated the premises, he layered my own juices across anything that might still be dry on my genitalia and used the faintest and then most pointed touches — and occasional torment with the edge of a fingernail — to my throbbing clit, which felt to me like it had grown to the size of a baseball.

I moved and twisted against the ropes as much as I could, begging for more, begging for the whole package. But as my writhing, and my mewing and my gasps, accelerated the son-of-a-bitch just stopped. Just fucking stopped.

I panted. My whole body drummed with the rhythm of my racing heart, and at the same time, I worried that if he didn't do something more soon I would burst into tears.

Which was not the release I had wanted when I came. I can cry in disappointment at home with some discounted organic popcorn and my friends on Hulu or Netflix.

I heard the clatter of the glass again. The room had fallen so silent I swear I could hear him swallow as he refreshed himself from the glass. The familiar salty scents of my arousal filled the room.

"You okay?" he asked, always a gentleman.

"No, motherfucker. Get on with it."

He chuckled. I might have added another thirty minutes to my torment. A door opened. A door closed. I could do nothing but shake. It might have been anticipation. It might have been fear. And then, my ears detected a familiar but new-to-this scenario sound, a hiss and a rattle. The bastard had jacked the air conditioning.

I thrashed against the ropes now as my flesh tightened against the drop in temperature. The cold gust focused on my hot and messy cunt. I groaned. He had positioned me to face the damn vent. I bore down and bit my lips together to keep from fighting my restraints. I recognized another sound. The toilet seat hit the tank and a hearty stream of piss, hot piss, hit the bowl. I fumed inwardly.

Johnny washed his hands, and I heard faint humming. Not the air conditioning or the toilet, but happy human singing. I sighed. The gesture relaxed my body.

He crept back into the room. Renewed ice clatter followed his footsteps so he must have topped off the ice water. I sensed his movement toward the nightstand, and I anticipated what he might do next once he put the glass in its place.

And what happened was nothing like what I had wished for; he pressed that icy glass hard against my pussy. I screamed and then whimpered as my body spasmed in shivers.

The glass disappeared. The air conditioning stopped. My strained noises though, they continued. Johnny kissed my forehead and ran his fingers through my hair.

"There, there my sweet good girl," he said.

My tension melted with his words. Like I said, the man understood my thresholds. Stillness. Silence.

And moments after, fingers filled me once again. Nothing pressing against outside me this time, but pounding regular strokes inside. Whatever was happening this time, stretched me, challenged me, made my hips arch. He licked my clit as more pressure teased me inside, an intoxicating blend of movement and fullness. Somehow, something forced my walls wider, easing toward my entrance and extending somewhere in me that had never been touched and maneuvered like this. Giggles tumbled from my lips.

The sensation pulled down toward my gateway, leaving hollowness behind and a strange twist triggered waves of initial orgasm in places I did not know. There was a gentle rapidness to Johnny's attentions, and the pattern; I had to wonder if he had thrust his whole fist into my vagina.

I had harbored that fantasy for a long time, ever since a work colleague and I discovered we had the same gynecologist. She complained about our doctor's large hands, something I had never noticed. Johnny loved exploring my fantasies from PIV fucking while wearing weighted anal plugs or releasing his cock on a public hiking trail in the woods and devoting myself to its worship.

The giggles built into laughter which Johnny correctly interpreted as my approaching ultimate delight. If you could drive a fist into a pussy like a piston in a high powered engine while still using every digit to memorize inside of its tight canal, that's what Johnny did, twisting and pumping with hydraulic precision.

I know — you have to be thinking, "he HAD to be hurting her" — and I suppose you're right, but my warm spots reignite even now, years later, to think of the intensity and the stretching. The closest thing I can compare it to is the stress of a heavy lift in the gym, when you push through while your muscles protest it's too much. You ignore them and you make the lift, and endorphins take over and you don't remember a single second of pain so you repeat the lift.

I burst into orgasm from the inside out, the rippling below my navel transforming into tremors that spanned into my fingers and toes, which I would have curled and snarled into the sheets if I hadn't been so carefully restrained. I cackled with the intoxication of it all, laughing until the spasms of Johnny's efforts become too much, which he sensed as I choked on my laughter, unable to process my own breath.

And when he removed his arm from my body, I felt a release as if I were a balloon that popped, and like that balloon, I deflated in exhaustion and joy. As my body continued to process waves of energy I laughed quietly now, my center hollow and gaping.

Johnny laughed, too, as he adroitly removed the blindfold. The room never seemed so vivid and awash with sun. A coating of my own making covered his left arm to the elbow. He untied me, cautioned me to rest as he scurried off to wash.

I stayed motionless until he returned, my smells still evident upon him. He scooped me into his arms and held me as we both giggled and caressed each other. He held me as I sipped what remained of the water, then he brought me one of his t-shirts which hung across my frame like a dress. He delivered ice cream to me in bed, which I ate while he massaged my feet and calves to ensure no muscles had cramped during my confinement.

As if that weren't enough, he fingered me and ate me out until I came several more times. He offered easy, restful orgasms as recovery for the one that ripped my soul from my body and transported me to a place of peace.

He insisted I have another glass of water, and made me a pea-
nut butter and jelly sandwich, before I could put on my clothes.
As I pulled my pants over my hips, he stopped me with a gesture.
Johnny slipped my pants to my ankles, bent me over his knee,
and swatted my bare ass with his hand. He reached to the bedside
table, and before I knew it, he had a wooden ruler which he used
to mark my already red cheeks.

"So you have bruises to remember this," he said.

As if I could forget. I reached for my pants, and again he
stopped me. He kissed me, softly, not parting my lips, and sat me
on his lap like a child, but spread my legs over his thighs like the
woman I was.

And he snapped the ruler across my clit. He liked the number
seven. So as soon as he uttered the first count, I knew when and
how this would end. His left hand expertly scored my aching clit
with the ruler as his right hand reached across me and pinched my
nipple, closing tightest as the pain of the clit-paddle hit.

By three, I had tears in my eyes but no strength to fight. By
four, I hollered, unable to hold it in.

"You need water?" He asked as he continued to torment the
nipple awaiting my response.

"No," I said, harsher than I intended, full of defiance.

"Good," he said. The word left his lips at the same time five
struck.

Six released the tears from my eyes. And seven — landing as
he extended my nipple outward with a strain I thought might rip
it off — made me orgasm that final time.

The world went white.

Bedpost

by Angie Ravenstone

The other young women ushered Cassidy into a luscious bedroom covered in velvet and satin, deep purples and bleeding red. They wore sheer tops, more like bathing suit cover-ups, nothing underneath, nothing to hide their perky breasts and the various colors of their nipples. They floated around the room like the Brides of Dracula.

They took her coat, and as one of them hung it in the closet, their soft hands worked together to peel away every stitch of clothing on her body. It happened fluidly as one of the women kissed her, the woman's plump lips parting hers and allowing their tongues to dance and spar.

She couldn't even tell when the clothes were gone, because hands kept caressing her, tongues kept exploring her. One woman pulled her legs apart as two more sat before her on their knees, grasping one leg each. Hands separated her ass cheeks and someone's tongue probed her tight star. She trembled with the anticipation of it all as the women guided her nude body to the bed and tied her wrists and ankles with silky rope.

Once they had secured her to the bedposts, the leader of the women entered the room. She wore a massive cloak, but nothing else except for a feathered mask across her eyes and violet lipstick.

The woman closest to the leader approached the bedpost on the left side of the footboard and unscrewed the ornate, swirled knob that adorned it. She twisted and twisted with quite some heft as the metal finally came off of the bed. The ornament at the top of the bedpost exceeded the size of the woman's fist, the tip small and shaped like a strawberry but expanding into an over-sized grenade before reducing its size again and swelling a final time at the flange.

One of the other women approached the leader and reapplied her vivid lipstick. The leader then crawled upon Cassidy as she laid spread-eagle on the bed. She covered Cassidy's vulva with purple lip prints and smears as she kissed her way to Cassidy's personal depths. One of the others applied a blindfold to Cassidy. She wriggled against her restraints and moaned against the leader's lips until everything suddenly stopped.

The leader no longer joined Cassidy in bed.

"You know what happens next, right?" the leader said.

"Yes," Cassidy choked out, her mouth dry from the guttural sounds she'd been making.

The room went silent. Terrifyingly silent.

"We cannot proceed until you acknowledge and consent to the specific actions we intend to take."

"I want you to fuck me," Cassidy said. "I want you to fill my pussy with whatever you deem fit."

With that, someone slid a rippled, cold object into her cunt. It stretched her as they forced it slowly deeper inside, its temperature a construct to the heat her body created. It pushed, and pushed, feeling fatter and fatter, until suddenly her tunnel felt like it collapsed around it. And the wide lip pressed against her exterior.

A gasp escaped her. They must have interpreted this as a sign, and whoever controlled the item inside of her used the opportunity to twist it, a half-circle to the left then a rapid turn to the right. Occasionally a swirl all the way around. The grooves and the bubbled texture, the object's large size and unyielding metal, teased her insides in a way that a man never could, no human could ever be so precise and eternal.

Then, whoever controlled the makeshift dildo extracted it just enough to release and rearrange the pressure, before pumping it into her like the pseudo-penis they intended it to be. With each motion, Cassidy lurched into it, getting accustomed to the bulbous and ridged sensation, and her tormentors pushed deeper into her, tipping and twirling and fucking.

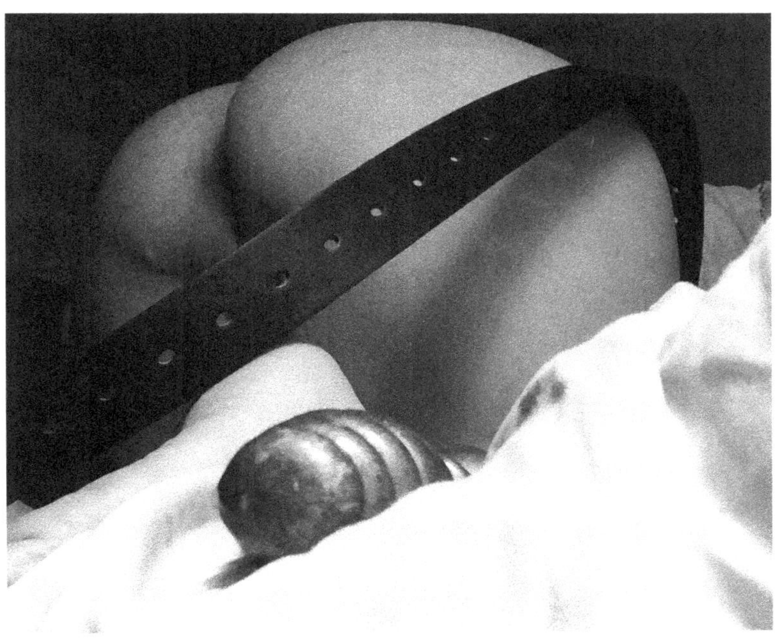

Her pussy released loud sucking noises due to the size of the object, and Cassidy writhed with each new and more rapid probe. When she moved just right the largest, fullest, grooviest section of the item — which had to be the bedpost, did it not? — struck something inside her that made her abdomen tight and sent timid shocks toward her upper thighs. Her nipples tingled. She needed more of that. She needed some much more of that.

"Cassidy," the leader's familiar voice said, "Are you okay?"

Whoever guided the bedpost slowed to a subtle tickle, the strawberry tip teasing her entrance. Cassidy howled in frustration.

"If you don't remember the safe word, you can always use the color system."

"I need you to finish what you started," Cassidy said.

The bedpost shot forcefully into Cassidy's needy hole, Cassidy clenched upon it and thrashed against her ropes attempting to close her thighs as the bedpost brutally used her vagina, its unique shapes and textures hitting every erogenous tissue inside of her, pain welling in her depths, so bad she couldn't tell if it were from discomfort or from pleasure.

Cassidy felt the prickly heat behind her belly button, then into her core, emanating out into her arms and her legs, as her toes curled and her hips arched. She bellowed as the power of the orgasm caused her body to shake violently and tears rolled from her eyes.

The bedpost was removed. The other women quickly unbound her, wiped her sweat, and held her. They took away the blindfold and massaged her wrists and ankles. Another woman gave her a glass of water.

And then the leader smiled, and said, "Who's next?"

Everyone's hands shot up, except for Cassidy, who replied, "it's my turn, right? Now I get to fuck you into oblivion."

The leader slipped off her mask, smirking, revealing dancing blue eyes with just a hint of devilishness.

"As you wish."

Cassidy climbed to the end of the bed, still shaky, unsteady on her knees. She kissed the leader while holding her hair a little too hard. When they broke apart, she took the leader's cloak and donned it.

"On the bed, bitch," she said. "You're mine now."

When Lust Can Heal

A Fashion and Fiends erotic story
By Angel Ackerman

Paris, 2020.

Jacqueline, now at-home with her family after another chaotic day at Val-de-Grâce arguing with men who outranked her, studied medical reports on Étienne's bed lit by his posh lamp with the crystal base and the rich lavender shade. She found this room inviting and cozy, and after so many late night heart-to-hearts with a man who had always been in her life, it no longer felt like a bedroom but a sanctuary. Étienne's son, Alèxandre, her nephew, had gone for a walk with his cousins, as sadly the pandemic limited their teenaged social interactions to each other.

Étienne had prepared a lovely dinner for them all, and had insisted she not worry about the cleaning, that he would do it. So she came into this room, with her service dog and some reading on the virus to decide for herself how to keep her family and patients safe. After decades of practicing military medicine, she mistrusted the information disseminated to the public perhaps more than anyone. But the reports passed around by the Army Health Services might be even more misleading. Jacqueline spent most of her free time knee deep in medical databases (which depending on the leg, might not be that deep, she joked to herself) and neck deep in paper.

She had nowhere else to go right now, pandemic raging and their family plagued (pun intended?) by tragedy after tragedy. At least here, in her brother-in-law's bedroom, the closest photograph to her featured her sister. Basilie always looked beautiful and confident, primarily because of the attention Étienne gave her, serving as her stylist and showing the world everything he loved about her. What woman wouldn't blossom under the devotion of a world famous fashion designer?

Jacqueline told the rowdy teenagers and her extended family of sisters and their units that she retreated to this room for solitude and quiet. As the youngest of five sisters, Jacqueline had a knack for escape. Honestly, though Jacqueline would never admit this to anyone, not even Étienne, she favored this room because she could feel her sister here, feel her sister's presence lingering.

And she missed her sister so much.

She had never been close to their mother. None of their other sisters had the same staid maturity as Basilie. Youngest and oldest. They were the outliers in their own way. Basilie, as the first child in the clan, always looked out for Jacqueline — and Jacqueline, as the baby, ignored most of her advice.

Étienne approached from the kitchen. He hovered in the doorway. She met his gaze with that certain look that asked why he might be staring. He smiled. A surprised look of concentration flashed into his eyes and their contact broke.

"Étienne?"

He didn't respond.

"You okay?"

Still nothing. He shifted his weight, mentally somewhere else.

"Étienne?" she repeated. "I'm asking as a doctor this time."

He murmured and snapped from whatever had caused his reverie.

"Petite Jacqueline," he said in a voice that sounded distant. An unnatural beat followed. "I am... hard."

"Oh?" she replied, still lost in doctor mode.

She placed her book on the nighttime table and made eye contact with her sister as she stood behind the frame. She then glanced to Étienne. Sure enough, she now noticed a change in the drape of his pants.

"Because of me?" she asked him.

He chuckled and awkwardly shifted his weight again as if jiggling things around might relieve the pressure.

"A little," he said. "When I turned the corner and looked in here, you very much resembled Zelie."

She chuckled this time. "I don't look anything like my sister."

He so clearly didn't know how to react to Jacqueline's unwavering gaze. Whatever, she thought, as a woman surrounded by soldiers every day, she found it only fair that a man experience an uncomfortable, objectifying stare.

"No," he agreed, running his hand not-so-discreetly across the front of his pants. And a familiar zing shot across Jacqueline's lower abdomen. "It was just the book, and the papers, and the posture. It brought me back."

A man unapologetically touching his cock always stirred her latent horniness, and apparently a woman surrounded by books and papers did something to him. She surveyed the documents scattered across her bed and almost laughed. The Golden Retriever slept peacefully on her other side. Her doctor's brain suddenly saw the situation differently.

Fuck you, medical training, she thought to herself, because here was a sweet and vulnerable man, whom all her sisters adored and had chattered about in their bedrooms even before Basilie dated him. His father had been her father's tailor, and his mother had laundered her father's shirts, and he himself had been her sister Claire's competitive ballroom dancing partner for most of their childhood. Jacqueline knew many sides of this man.

"Is that something you think you're ready for?" she asked.

"It's been more than 15 years," he said.

Étienne married Basilie when Jacqueline was ten. And for most of their adult lives, he and Basilie had this intense but dramatic on-again, off-again marriage. They were officially divorced but still madly in love when they miraculously conceived Alèxandre in their forties. But the Universe went a little haywire — Étienne got coerced and abducted by a psychopathic supermodel and to save him, Basilie sacrificed herself. And to save his reputation, Jacqueline cashed in some favors with the brass, accepting a UN assignment in Afghanistan in exchange for a medal and recognition of Étienne's heroic deeds. She wished she could say some of those decisions turned out to be the "right ones."

"Wow," she replied. "I know that shouldn't surprise me, because… the kids… but yes, it has."

"I didn't know if it would ever happen again."

He gestured very mildly toward the front of his khakis. She looked directly into his eyes.

Because of the family relations, she shouldn't have done it. But she was the first on scene that day, when they rescued Étienne and lost her sister. Étienne at that moment was malnourished, trembling, filthy, clutching an underdeveloped newborn to his chest (which was not Alèxandre, but a half-sibling but that was still unclear at that time). Because of her work in Africa, in war zones, post incidents where soldiers or terrorists or just plain old men did their disgusting deeds, Jacqueline recognized immediately the layers of bruising on his wrists, the spots on his neck, the jagged stance of his obviously fucked up fingers, and the emptiness behind his eyes. She had planned to maintain protocol and have someone else do it, but the man had obviously been through torture and when he begged her not to let anyone else touch him, she had no choice but to perform an assessment of his injuries herself. Those memories froze her desire, but as she looked at him, she could see he was not in the past.

"You have worked on a lot. We've shared a lot. You did more for me than anyone after my own trauma," she said. "So, if you want… I mean, I will… I could… I haven't myself since my husband died… but, I'm not going to pressure you. After everything, you need to be in control of this experience. And I wouldn't expect… well… fireworks?"

He laughed and swung his curly bangs from his face.

"You wouldn't find that weird?" he asked.

"Sleeping with my widower brother-in-law? No," she said without hesitation.

"You just propositioned me in the most mechanical way I've ever heard," he said.

"Oh come on," she said. "You know until we got married we were both the biggest whores in our families."

He chuckled. His face expressed an ease that made her look at him in a new way.

"But you need to be emotionally ready," she warned. "This could be harder than you think."

Étienne fought a laugh that twisted his lips into a smirk. "I certainly hope so."

That didn't make sense, she thought. Then, she got the joke. Men. "I meant psychologically triggering."

"Yes, Doctor," he said, blatantly mocking her. "I'm aware of my history of sexual assault. But hey, we both have PTSD. So who knows what will happen."

Her service dog jumped off the bed.

"Well, the dog thinks we should do it," she said.

He moved closer to her.

"May I kiss you?" he asked.

"That might be a good place to start."

He closed the gap between them, but then stumbled, and regained his footing. He shook his head. Directing her attention to the floor, she realized he had tripped over her prosthetic.

"I'm used to Alèx leaving his shoes lying around," Étienne remarked. "But that's the first time I ever fell over a foot."

"Sorry," she said. "I went ahead and got comfortable. It gets bulky after a long day."

His legs pressed against her knees, as he cupped her cheeks with his hands and pushed her hair behind her ears. She tilted her face toward him and he lowered his lips. Feeling the warmth of another body approach her and lean against her transported her to happier and more easygoing times. God, how just that feeling of someone else's skin against her stirred her sleeping desires.

And when their mouths touched, she suddenly understood how deeply he cared for her. There was an easy rhythm and a desperation underlying it. He always smelled delicious, so the comfort in his aroma circling her came as no surprise. His lips were as soft as his perfect hands. His face hinted at five o-clock shadow. His taste landed as vibrant as the sweet dessert cordial he offered her after dinner. His gentle kiss asked her to open her body to him, nothing brutal or demanding about it, but a kiss of appreciation and joy celebrating the moment. His tongue explored her with a delicacy and skill that spoke of all his life experience. It clearly said, "I know how to get to you."

He slowly teased himself away, lips dancing across lips, but she broke the embrace abruptly.

"Jacqueline?" he said. "Is something wrong?"

"No," she said, but her mind buzzed with conflicting messages that the kiss had shared with her, the needs of a widow who lost her husband two years prior, the concerns of a doctor aware of how heavy this situation was, and the fear of a sister who wanted to make the right decision.

"I never realized," she said, "that you cared for me so much."

"I do," he said, "and I don't think I realized it until now."

"You haven't done that in fifteen years?" she asked.

He stifled a sound and it came out of his nose as a cute exhale as his cheeks blushed.

"No."

"Well, you haven't forgotten how," she said.

Étienne smiled, and it was that wide, goofy, affable grin that she attributed to him. As if twenty years had slipped away and they were young again.

"I'm not a docile lover," Jacqueline said, in a whispered formal tone — bedroom doctor voice? she wondered — "but I'm going to follow your lead, and you can use my body to find your way back."

His eyes twinkled, but they also blinked away a tear. "Thank you."

"Étienne, I'm serious," she said. "I have no expectations, just see how it feels. If you decide you don't want to, that's okay, too."

He kissed her again. She relaxed into it and felt his hands cascade to her shoulders, then down her arms, and to her rib cage. When she came into the room earlier, she had removed her bulky military jacket. The heat of his strong hands permeated the stiff uniform blouse. The pressure and combination of body heat against fabric fueled her in a way she had almost forgotten.

He broke the kiss and gingerly unbuttoned the blouse, even more carefully shrugging it off her shoulders. He blinked, or maybe squinted, and then started to trace the ink on her outer shoulders.

"I knew you had tattoos," he said, his fingers on the rod of Asclepius. His hand move to the vines across her belly, also riddled with scars. "But…"

His fingertips bounced from leaf to leaf.

"I did not know…" he muttered.

She said nothing. He did not need to know that until a certain point in her career she added another leaf to the vine every time she lost one of her patients, every leaf was a soldier, usually some fearless twenty-year-old, who would never go home. And he didn't ask about the flags on her right arm, from shoulder to elbow, one for every country she'd served in.

Étienne removed his shirt, and his undershirt. He stepped between her knees and guided her further across the bed and atop the papers.

She soon forgot the reports, noticing his firmness, quite admirable for a man his age. He was at least ten years her senior. His hands brushed their way across her body and finished undressing her. Well, everything except her panties. Her good leg dangled over the edge of the bed and other knee and residual limb gripped the top of the mattress.

"May I undress you?" she asked.

He inhaled softly through his nose.

"Yes," he answered.

He trembled as she unwound his belt, very deliberately. She could see his unwavering focus on her face as he fought to stay in the moment. She flung the belt across the room, which caused a grimace to cross his face. She instinctively seized his arm to check his pulse, which made him flinch. She noticed the even rise and fall of his chest and she realized her mistake. He hadn't thought she was about to beat him with the belt.

"What?" she said playfully, as she released his wrist. "If you want me to put it someplace nicely I either have to hop or put my leg back on."

He laughed and took a step back from the bed. She laid her hands on his hips.

"Are you okay?" she asked.

"Very much so," he replied.

She unbuttoned his fly and slowly lowered the zipper. "Still okay?"

He nodded. Those curls flopped as he did. She pulled his pants down his legs, keeping her hands to his sides. They fell.

"Keep going?" she asked.

"Yes, please."

Jacqueline didn't know how his past experiences with sexual assault would impact him, and from her own PTSD she had learned that sometimes the wrong sound could freeze her — so how could she expect Étienne to allow a woman to touch him and not flashback to the trauma in some way?

She laughed to herself as she compared her clinical approach to Étienne to how Philomé probably dealt with her, god rest his immortal soul. But Philomé was a psychiatrist and she wasn't sure she had the finesse to handle this as well as he would have. And she had been blown up by an IED, not raped.

She peeled the waistband of his perfect Charvet boxers, belonging to a man who enjoyed opulence and craftsmanship, and freed his erection, which despite its solidness couldn't quite stand as proudly as a young man's cock. But still… It was longer than most and quick thick, healthy coloring that confirmed good blood flow, a gentle pulsing rhythm as it waited, and precious drops of first juices that she longed to taste. He remained well-groomed and even now smelled clean and deliciously aroused.

"Jacqueline, are you assessing my penis?"

"Actually, yes," she said. "And you have a nice one."

"Thank you, Doctor Saint-Ebène. I've always enjoyed it."

She had to smile at his humor. He stood naked before her, still quite handsome, not even really gray. His stray tufts of chest hair had a wiry stiffness to them, but he was a trim man who, though he didn't really exercise or have the rock hard body of her deceased husband, stayed active enough to remain average.

There was an underlying tension in his stance. His body language suggested a level of fear or perhaps suppression. He didn't seem wholly present. The dog, who had moved to the floor, raised his head. He felt it, too. Or maybe he merely noticed her concern.

"Étienne," she cooed. "You are not entirely with me."

He said nothing, but stood like a statue, and Jacqueline thought she noticed a hint of deflation in his hard-on.

"Étienne," she said. "Listen to me."

She placed her hands on his upper arms.

"You are in control of this whole experience, and I need you to do something."

His eyes moved downward to meet her.

"Hit me," she said. "Slap me as hard as you fucking can right across the face."

His lips parted as his chin dropped. Her statement broke whatever trance he had been in.

"Hell, yeah," she said. "You never had any sort of justice or revenge for what happened to you. So hit me. Hit me as if I were her, let some of that anger and resentment out."

"I… don't want… to hurt you," he said.

"You won't," she said. "But you need to let some of it go."

He closed his eyes. He inhaled through his nose and she watched his chest expand. And fluidly, without hesitation, he raised his right arm and slapped his palm across her cheek with a force that jerked her chin past her opposing shoulder. The flesh stung. He opened his eyes as she gave her head a little shake. Her pussy burned more than she liked to admit, and she now sat in a puddle. He shoved her down, pulled her panties to the slide, and slammed his thick cock into her violently. The papers crinkled and the bed groaned under their weight and his force. She wrapped her arms loosely around his back, not wishing to restrain him and hooked her asymmetrical legs over his hips as best she could.

He growled as he used her, and she — not accustomed to being the lie there and no nothing type — focused on a visual monitoring of his vitals, not quite being able to disconnect her concern for his safely, and treasured this submissive use of her body, allowing this man the freedom to reclaim his own sexuality and express his rage in a way she secretly adored. Jacqueline had a masochistic streak that hadn't seen the light of day since before her accident. The pressure and friction of

Étienne's groin tearing into her bordered on violence, but she reveled in absorbing his emotional pain with her physical body.

"Étienne, you're no longer the victim, don't hold back," she whispered into his ear.

He gazed into her eyes with a possessed look, a demon welling from within him. He moved his hands from the bed to her shoulders, one meaty palm engaged on each and he pinned her, limiting her range of motion, pressing into the bone. And he continued to fuck her viciously, pounding parts of her vagina that even a doctor hadn't checked in years.

And what did it say about her that her toes started to curl, her respirations increased, her thighs tingled and her belly threatened to ripple? She couldn't believe — and the thought heightened her arousal — that after 15 coitus-free years and at 60-years-old this man could animalistically pummel her guts. His hands slipped, and he fell, knocking some breath out of her. He readjusted, but kept his cock entrenched. The pause allowed her to feel its throbbing inside her. It also cooled her potential orgasm. Her heart raced. She had sweat on her brow. And there was a part of her, a shamed part of her, that did not want to show Étienne that she would come from this rough, hateful romp.

And then, Étienne lowered his head, grabbed her nipple with his teeth and pulled. She yelped, and he resumed his rutting, awkwardly curled to keep pressure on the nipple without breaking his stride. She tilted her face toward him, and kissed his head. He released her breast, met her eyes, and relaxed into a gentler pace. He screamed out as his body rocketed into orgasm and his cock exploded as powerfully as the whole experience had gone. He wilted inside her, a sensation she loved, as the papers on the bed turned mushy. Hot, sticky fluids covered their groins, stomachs and thighs.

As they extricated their limbs, Étienne traced the scars on her body, the raised stars from shrapnel, the deep lines from surgeries, even the long-healed bullet wound near her breast. He trailed a hand to her residual limb.

"Your glass eye freaks me out, but your leg, it just ends. I expected it to be fleshier."

"It was, in the beginning."

"I still feel responsible," he said.

"Don't," she said. "Those bastards would have found a way to send me to Afghanistan regardless of how and when. As for what happened, the Taliban didn't like the women's clinic. That has nothing to do with you."

This time she kissed him. She placed her hand against his chest and felt his heartbeat reverberate as she praised him with her mouth, wondering how and if she could ask him to keep going, to let her finish, or if that might be too much pressure. His hand dipped toward her sloppy, used pussy, danced across her swollen lips and found her engorged clit.

A door closed at the other end of the apartment. The children — the teenagers — had returned home. They headed into the kitchen, probably for snacks and/or drinks. The refrigerator door opened.

"Papa!" Alexandre called. "We're home."

Jacqueline chuckled. "Well, now, we probably should have planned that more carefully."

Étienne also chuckled and pointed to the bathroom adjoining the bedroom.

"Do you want to…"

"Sure," Jacqueline said, "can you pass me my leg?"

He did as she asked. She rummaged around the bed for her uniform. He quickly donned clothes and tucked his shirt into his pants. She layered her liner onto her residual limb, and popped the stump into her prosthetic.

"Hey kids," Étienne yelled. "Anybody want to go bowling?"

"Bowling?" Jacqueline replied.

Étienne threw up his hands in a dramatic, flustered gesture. "It was all I could think of."

"Since when do we bowl?" Alèxandre replied.

"Give me your jacket," Étienne demanded.

Jacqueline pointed to the lump on the floor. Étienne seized the jacket and ripped off a button.

"Étienne," she called to him. "We're going to have to talk about this."

"Yes," he said. "I hope… I did not harm you."

"Oh God no," she assured him with a wave and a smirk.

He grabbed a needle and thread from the sewing kit he always had nearby and walked into the hall.

"I'll finish repairing this button for you, Jacqueline," he said loudly as he turned toward the living room.

Jacqueline shook her head. Étienne leaned into the bedroom and looked at her from over his shoulder.

"Thank you, Jacqueline."

THEMES: 69, ass play, chastity cage, dildo worship, dominance/submission, facial, girdle fetish, hand job, long-distance, packing, piercings, prostate massage, spanking

On The Tenth Night With Miss O.

By W.S. E'das

"I wanna come, Miss O. I wanna come so bad."

"I know, baby, I know, but you're doing so good. Another three days, I know you can do it."

"Please, please, please let me out now. Please."

"Do you really want that baby, really? I mean, really, really? I'll unlock you right now, sure. But you know you don't want me to. You know I want this for you. You know I know you can do this. Just think how incredible it will feel when I finally take this cage off you and jerk you off. How much you'll come, how incredible your balls will feel when you finally release. How we will both know you did it, made all the way through the ten days… I'll even tickle your asshole with my finger just the way you like."

"Oh, Miss O.!"

"Then, I can get on you and ride your cock an hour later. You'll be able to last as long as I need you to, having just had that big explosion. It will be perfect. So, let's not, okay? I mean, I will release you right now if this is really what you want, but you don't really want me to, do you?"

"Noooo."

* * * *

God-awfully dirty-minded from the jump with me, the first time Octavia and I met, after months of chatting online and her coming into town from her Atlanta home for a business meeting, we kissed a quick hello. Then, I pulled her back into her hotel room, sat on her bed, skirted her across my knee as she giggled-moaned to me spanking the back of her jeans ten high hard swats, as I had threatened to do if we ever met. By the time we were huddled in the cab popping from one busy Manhattan tourist trap to another that day, we were all but dry humping in the backseat, where I once again spanked her big ass so the cab driver could hear.

That night, I'd lay the fleshy lady naked and face up on her hotel bed, take her hair brush to her bald pussy, and smack her thick wet lips so hard she pretty much squirted across the room while pleading for "more, more, more."

From that first weekend, the pale-skinned, thirty-eight-year-old and I pretty much attacked one another every chance we got together. Other than with Beth, a petite and busty brunette I had dated a half a decade before, I had never been so sexually compatible with a woman, at least not in my most recent memory, and the green-eyed lady and I began spending hours on the phone, getting each other off, or, when we could manage it, visiting each other and conjuring some sure heated craziness.

I'd make Octavia spank herself hard and long over hour-long phone chats, then order her insert her obscenely large dildo as she'd agree to all kinds of naughty scenarios I'd lay out before her.

She, in turn, would coo all kinds of soft promises to me as she had me close my eyes, imagine her next to me, jerking my cock until I blew in her face, something she especially seemed to like. I even called her once when her younger friend Victoria was visiting, a slender brunette who flitted and flirted her seeming bisexuality by trying to get Octavia to notice her super long legs and high ass.

On this occasion, Octavia put her cell on speaker, and we convinced sweet Victoria that she was in need of an over-the-knee, bare-assed spanking. Slowly, the twenty-six-year-old complied, mainly because it was Octavia about to do the swatting, and I had Octavia take pictures of Victoria's apple-red bottom after she got through with it that night. Later we both masturbated over Octavia detailing what else she had done to Victoria after I had disconnected the call.

Octavia was bi.

It's ironic when I think back on Octavia and me, how pretty much through our long-distance relationship, I had begun as the stern dominant, even more so than I ever had with Beth. It made me so fucking horny to snap my fingers and have the pale-skinned chubby girl strip for me, no matter when or where, to smack her wide white rear a scarlet red, to make her come in her pants just by repeating "punishment, punishment" in her ear. I loved being her dom so much I almost didn't get around to having her dominate me.

Almost.

Octavia had been strictly dominant, often sternly so, with every woman she had ever been with. Through some passing moments in college as well as her affair with a married lady and a few of her 'closer' girlfriends, in her homosexual canoodling, Octavia spanked and dildoed, ordered her women to dress as she wanted, 'forced' girlfriends to be 'used' by others, and pretty much led her affairs nearly one hundred percent of the time. Relating this past to me, of course, endeared the big girl to me even more… as well as giving me lots of fodder to masturbate over.

But by the time we met, Octavia had quieted her wily ways (somewhat) and was undoubtedly more discerning and discreet when she picked partners in her little city. As I suspected though, once she began to consider that I indeed wanted to submit to her, Octavia advised me of specific parameters of what she would and would not entertain as a top… with a man. Interestingly, while she didn't seem to have any specifics to her submission, she did when dominating guys, the few times she admitted that she had.

Firstly, Octavia liked to be called 'Miss O.' when dominating me and what this conjured for me during sex play, made me crazy. I had no real care for roleplay, but I'd take a nurturing matter-of-fact domina over a leather-clad kitten delivering a whipping was what I most wanted. Calling her Miss O. as much set the moment as one where the pretty chubby-cheeked woman was in sure dom mode as made me feel that I was answering with my "sweet little ass" (Octavia's words not mine) to a sure comeuppance.

Secondly, I noticed that on the phone or in person, Octavia would let slip an ever-so-slight southern-accented lilt to her voice when starting to get strident with me. She had grown up pretty much close to where she still lived in Atlanta, so it made sense she'd still have some vestige of this more pronounced accent. Octavia claimed she wasn't consciously aware of the change in her speech, coming as it did when we were well into the throes of her topping me; all I knew was the slight change in her voice, coming as it did naturally, and only when she was Miss O., yet again, not in the guise of true roleplay, made me fucking insane.

And thirdly — and something that spoke to her deep nurturing nature — the lady would never entertain or layout scenarios that hinted at true humiliation when dominating me.

Even though I assured Octavia that I felt infinitely safe with her and damn well-liked to have my cock size assessed or be made to eat my cum, she explained that being a Southern lady through and through, she couldn't skirt around any play that she felt even hinted at degrading a man.

Teasing, denying, even setting in some righteous sexual dread was all well and good, but she drew the line in her cute, little curly-haired noggin' over certain things. For example, when she coaxed me to wear a pair of her red panties on my first visit to her home, she had me show her friend Karen what I had on, but only by requesting I lift the lacy hip of the underwear over my jeans. As much as I would have loved to have revealed my cock, balls, and ass in the tight, lacy undies, Octavia wouldn't traipse into what she felt would be humiliating.

These limits though didn't make her domination any less potent.

Starting by spanking me with her hairbrush or making me do the same to myself when we talked on the phone, Octavia came to dom me in a whole host of delicious ways. As befit her crafty little mind, each scenario, whether we just talked about it, or it happened, or we set up the possibility of it occurring, was as unnerving as it was thrilling.

On her third visit to me, just about when she began to flip as much to dominant as submissive, Octavia and I bought fleet enemas at my local drug store. We never got to use them, but the idea that we had them set us both to masturbate often over the phone after she left.

On our fifth visit, my second 'down' her way, once again, Octavia brought her bestie Karen into the mix, and spontaneously, so it was all the more exciting. The busty blonde had called as Octavia and I were starting to roll around, pulling each other's clothes off, and Octavia rolled out of bed, cell phone in hand, welcoming Karen to stop by.

"No, no, where you going, baby?" Octavia said to me, slipping her robe on. I had scooted to the edge of the bed. "Stay naked and hard right here. If Karen has to use the bathroom, I want you worrying she might walk down the hall, and if she does, I want her to see you."

"Octavia, I…"

She shot out of the room, and I stayed where I was, naked and undoubtedly hard, and five minutes later, the doorbell rang. Karen called a "hello" from the kitchen once Octavia let her in and told her where I was, but she never stepped down the hall. But I kept at myself, making sure I was rock hard as Octavia would have wanted, wonderfully worried and thrilled with the idea of Karen coming down the hall. Octavia later told me she had known Karen wasn't staying long and would have never had to use the bathroom. I guess I also knew deep down that given how she never truly wanted to humiliate me, Octavia wouldn't have had Karen see me so vulnerable (simply closing the bedroom door would have managed this), but we liked playing the possibility, it seemed.

At my house, the next time we saw one another in person, I made dinner one night. Octavia and I had gone out shopping for a few groceries an hour before, then spent the next few hours with me preparing the simple pasta meal, then eating. After we had cleaned up, the chubby girl led me to my couch, stood over me, and unzipped her jeans to flump a seven-inch dildo from her crotch. She had told me about the times her trio of her girlfriends had stepped out to a local bar, 'packing,' as they called it and although I wasn't sure if those stories were true, when Octavia pealed down her pants to show me the full strap-on harness, took a step, and grabbed the back of my head, I was inclined to believe her cock-tails.

I sucked her fake dick, something I had indeed thought of doing when faced with one before, as she began to tell me how she was finally going to fuck my ass as she had been wanting to do for a very long time. Although it had been a while for me and pegging, God knew I wanted this woman to take me that way.

But somehow, when I disengaged from giving her a faux blow-job, I managed to switch the moment's intent and got into doming Octavia. This is how things often ran with us, one slight deviation and if I got her bare ass close enough, as I did when I came off her cock, and she turned to flash me her big dimpled cheeks in the harness, I could be suddenly rushed with the idea of turning tables and dominating the lady.

And although there were moments that one of us would set the other into a specific kind of play — Octavia coming into the room wearing a corset, heels and choker, and red rubber gloves meant she was interested in tickling another full spill from me with her expert and unnerving prostate massage; me pulling the wooden spoon from my kitchen and meeting her dripping and wrapped in her towel just stepping out of the shower, certainly indicated who was going to get what from whom — most times, on the phone or in person, we just went where the mood took us.

I don't know if spanking was my 'gateway' kink (although I always suspected this to be the case), but man, it had led me down the rabbit hole of many fun diversions. Having a fantasy of being placed across a high bare lap as a young 20-something (and having been plenty) had progressed to me being scolded when I took swats. Having just the tip of one of my date's fingers sneak between my cheeks led to anal plugs and then pegging (albeit a few years down the line). Cock measuring, orgasm denial, and then eating my come had seemed like natural progressions for ever deeper submission and humiliation. From considering flirty fun college 'girls,' then women, then wanting to be attended to by a Mommy figure who might deliver a true comeuppance, my sexual awakening (and let's hope I would never be fully awake so as to always enjoy more and more play) had seen me through dating, marriage, divorce, dating again, and right then with Octavia, enjoying some of the most mind-blowing sex play I had ever had.

Chastity, then, seemed a natural next hurdle. I had been reading more and more about and masturbating over the idea. To have my cock caged, not able to jerk off, denied orgasm, under the control and lock-and-key of a lady, was thrilling for me to contemplate. And as I considered the possibility more and more, I realized here was a woman I could try it with.

* * * * *

When I landed at Octavia's for what was going to be our most extended visit yet, as usual, we just about got home from the airport before we were at each other. This time, we fell to Octavia's blue-and-white tile kitchen floor, ripped at each other's pants, and managed a spirited 69 as fast as we could lay next to one another and dive in. Octavia was always sure to "buff the good China," as she called it, enduring a very close bikini and anus waxing for our visits. Her perfect bare smoothness plus her "Christian" piercing (a tiny gold ball inserted at the very top of her pussy, just above the clitoral hood in the mons pubis) drove me absolutely wild whenever I got my mouth on her pink parts. As I lapped at her already soaking pussy, and she shook, sucked, and licked my cock, the woman took considered breaks lifting her mouth off me to breathlessly reveal a plan.

"I...I bought a cage for you," she said through a moan as I clutched her mottled ass cheeks and stayed where I was, circling the tip of my tongue across her engorging clit.

"Cock...lock," she attempted while I shuddered with her and tried to reason through what I thought she was saying before she swallowed me again and began coming as I flattened my tongue on her clit.

Sure, we had discussed her buying me a cage and one day locking up my cock, but as with the enemas, the ass-fucking, all we had said we were going to get to, and the plenty more we had, this was just another naughty idea Octavia, and I had entertained. Our problem (surely not a bad one to have) was that when we began to talk about anything sexual, in-person or over the phone, both of us usually got so charged we'd shuck, rattle and roll to mutual rushed orgasms. In the case of Octavia and me, talking about what we wanted to get to was sometimes even better than getting to it, if we did get to it at all.

But as she came a second time and popped my cock out her lips yet again, it seemed Octavia had her mind set on locking me up... and soon.

"After you come, now, you are going in," she said, arching back so I had to reposition on her hard tile.

Octavia said something more, but I was lost in coming as she began to jerk me off into her adorable face.

My balls and fevered brain considerably slaked as Octavia left me on the floor, I was looking up under cupboards and counter-tops, listening to the woman of the house grab whatever it was she had lifted herself off the tile to go get. Sure, I had heard what she had said, but right then, I was a little too post-cum relieved to settle my mind on what could have just been naughty sex talk. But when Octavia returned with a towel and what surely looked like a cock cage in her hand, I sat up, assured she was out to make good on her promise.

With me as much agreeing as fearing, my sometimes-girl first washed my cock and balls with the wet end of the towel and then dried me sufficiently (just about before I felt myself growing hard all over again), then got down on the floor next to me to fit the chastity cage (ring around my tight little balls, hard rubber cage cap, then tiny padlock) to my bait and tackle.

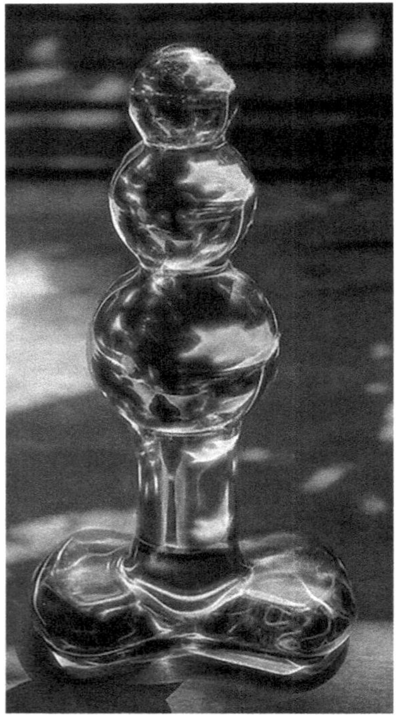

"I will take it off anytime you like," she said, leaning in to kiss me. "But let's see if you can take it for the whole time you are here."

Which was to be eleven days.

"I… erm …I," I said, looking down with her.

"I'll let you free on the tenth night, that would be hot I think, we can have our wildest time just before you leave."

If not for Octavia's consistent attention and God-awful, nearly polymorphous perverse sensibility, not being able to come or touch myself for a week-and-a half wouldn't have been as difficult. But while we visited with her friends, and Octavia came home from work lunchtime so we could catch a quick bite sitting on her high kitchen stools (stools I had sat on to pull Octavia across my lap) or me meeting her at the little coffee shop near her office, and late night cuddling watching the score of reality shows she considered her worst indulgence, my keymaster was either nibbling my neck, brushing up or completely writhing against me, presenting her bare ass for me to swat or lifting one of her heavy breasts to my face.

I knew it wasn't so much that I was caged that prompted the woman, she was rather horny most of the time anyway, but man, the frustration I felt those first few days skittled across my very skin, and Octavia seemed to groove to the sexual 'contact high' of my suffering. Which just made us both even hornier.

Already eating her pussy at a frequency I had never indulged in oral sex (Octavia really did have a spectacular vagina I couldn't seem to get enough of burying my face in), locking my dick up gave me even more impetus to get her off, and only get her off. I did come to consider that during that first week, she might, in her way, be growing as frustrated as me. Let's face it, this was a woman who damn well-liked a hard cock, in any which way, and surely, Octavia's pussy was "open for business."

But we were not fucking. She wasn't sucking my cock. And I pretty much didn't enter her with a finger or tongue tip. I didn't plan this last, per se, but when looking at my cage or strumming her fingers across my bulging balls or suffering cock, it was all Octavia could do not just to lie back and force my head into her crotch and my mouth on her pussy before she all but exploded.

I guess it was good for us both to suffer my chastity in our way.

* * * * *

"Oh, Miss O."

Octavia was lying beside me, roiling her left hip against my quivering leg; my suffering reaching a fever pitch this eighth night. The intense rush to get out and come had finally landed on me as heavy and hard as my overly sensitive balls felt, and I wanted more than anything to plow the woman hard with what I knew would only be a couple of minutes of fucking I was so full-to-bursting. Of course, it hadn't helped that Octavia had had my cocked cage in her mouth for a good percentage of the last hour. Somehow though, after my initial pleading and her soft assurances, we did manage to calm down to fall asleep in each other's arms.

Crisis averted. I really did want to stay in the cage for the duration.

Sure, this cock cage ordeal was unnerving, but what was getting to me more this visit, was how, once again, things felt so very right with Octavia. And I don't just mean sexually. Whether she was visiting me or I 'came in' to hang with her for a few days in her slightly artsy hilly little town, we seemed to be progressing into a more comfortable lock-step.

For all my randy ways and over-consideration of my kink needs, there had been only a handful of instances in my life where I wasn't thinking much about being someplace else or with someone else. When either in bed with Octavia or out at the little market in her town (that particular week walking through the wood-floored co-op had been incredibly challenging shucking my hips wearing the cage), I felt like I was supposed to be with Octavia, living a life with her. Moving in with her or she with me would have meant a drastic change, and when we weren't clawing at one another, thoughts of our relationship bliss were creeping in.

Of course, as I had with Beth years before, any woman I felt myself really coming to care for (save my ex-wife and look how that turned out, I often reminded my sworn-to-be-a-bachelor-forever self) I'd come to stomp the idea of monogamy and cohabitation down right quick. Hey, my cock was in a cage for two more nights, there was more to think about, right?

* * * * *

The house was completely dark, with some odd instrumental music playing off in the living room (Octavia had very eclectic tastes in music). I had stepped into the shower only ten minutes before, but in that time, she had turned all the lights off, lit a big candle on her dresser, and came out of her room in a girdle, heels, and pearls. She knew I had a thing, in addition to all my other things, for girdles (another fetish that had come to me over time and I could not explain). When I first admitted liking the utilitarian lingerie, Octavia had indeed surprised me once or twice by wearing a girdle under her clothes. But this special night, she presented herself to me dressed in it only.

"Come to me, baby," she said, that southern accent prominent. Affectation, real role-play — I didn't care. I stepped to her, dropping the towel.

"I am so proud of you, love," she said, leading me by hand into her living room, and sitting me on the couch.

"You have obeyed me in more ways than I could ever have dreamed," she said, kneeling and putting one hand under my purple testicles, the other slowly stroking down my aching mushroom cap under the thick plastic tip.

"It's time," she said, standing to turn to a small low table. Her hands popping off my cock I almost fell forward onto the floor. But Octavia was stepping back to me and kneeling again seconds later with my cock cage lock's key in her hand.

"Let's get this off..."

Bending slightly, she made quick work of unlocking the mini padlock and the ring under my balls. I huffed, again trying not to pitch forward as she extricated me entirely within seconds, and I lay there huffing as she placed cage, lock, and key to her side on the floor, leaned back, and let me breathe...in more ways than one.

Within a second, I was unfurling to half-mast.

"Now, not too much of this," she said, reaching for something else she had obviously retrieved when she had stepped for the key. She plucked a bottle of clear lube from the floor at her side.

"We don't want you going off prematurely," she said, squeezing a dollop of the clear strawberry-scented thick liquid into her right palm and then placing her wet hand on my hardening cock.

"Just to ease the chaffing, ya know?" she said, working me as I grew and my knees began to shake.

"Mmmm, mmm, it's been too long since I felt this in my hand."

"Or anywhere else," I sighed.

"Yes, sweetheart, yes," she moaned, working two hands down me.

"Ah, Oct… Miss O., I…" I clutched, swayed, and felt a tear coming to my eye.

"Okay, okay," she said, removing her hand, reaching for my towel, and wiping the lube off her hands and then my cock.

"Lay down, honey, on your back. It's time I gave you what you deserve."

As much as I was sure we'd get to humping, this big beautiful fleshy girl lying down next to me knew that what she had promised ten days ago was what I first wanted so much…. her usual expert handjob.

"You did so so good, so good," she continued making small circles with the tip of her fingers dead center of my testicles as she rolled up close to my side to make sure I felt the hard material of the girdle against my hip.

My cock was jumping, and I had to spread my legs to relieve the pressure.

"Thanks for helping me, Miss O."

"Yes, Miss O. helped you, yes," she said on her elbow, looking down at me intensely as she began to tap my balls.

"Oh, God, they hurt. They are so full."

"I know, I know," she cooed, leaned down, and kissed my lips.

I was pretty much fully rock-hard.

"Miss O.," I moaned as she increased the intensity of her tapping down below.

"Miss O!," I cried.

"Do you want to come now?" she asked, taking her hand from my balls and grabbing the base of my cock.

I began to hump the air.

"Yesss."

"We can prolong it even more if you like. I could send you home caged, then mail up the key."

"No, no, please, please!"

"Okay, okay," Octavia whispered and began to move her hand again, ever so slightly, just rubbing the base of my dick. She wiggled closer to get her knee up on my leg, her heel dangling so close I could sense more than feel it.

I had never endured play like this, engaged in such a systematic long-term submission, or known a woman to hold an interest in domming me for so long. I wasn't exactly sure if cock-caging was in my future, still, I realized what was roiling my arousal so much was as much the fact that my cock and balls were finally gloriously free as that this wonderful big girl had had the patience to endure the caging full term with me.

Octavia skittled down my body and put me in her mouth. This would arouse me, we both knew — how could it not — but ironically, keep me from coming... at least, at first. This girl was well aware that of all the ways I could get off. A blowjob, even the passionate cock-gobbling this woman managed, didn't usually bring me to orgasm. Sure, I was more than ready to explode, so her staying on me for even a small amount of time would most likely get me there. But her cool mouth on me, while feeling quite spectacular, put me in another zone where I was stimulated but just hard. We both knew I most wanted her to get me off by her hand, look at me, talk to me, and love me.

"So, so hard," Octavia said, coming up for air in a few seconds as I looked at her smile. "So, so hard."

"Yes, yes."

"Time to come," she continued getting up on her knees. Scooting up even closer, the girl again reached for the lube, "Splong-working," a dollop down her middle and first finger. She then pushed her hand under me.

Before I could even gulp, Octavia had both lubed fingers up my ass.

"Oh, Jesus. Oh sweet fucking Jesus!" I squealed as she pushed up, in and true, right to my prostate.

I couldn't help but bear down while I opened. Staring at Octavia's set, thin smile, her eyes so sympathetically peering at me, her fingers pinned me as much as her full caring.

"Ask me to let you release. Go ahead, ask me and I will let you."

My whole body was shuddering at that point. As much as I ached to come, was just on the verge to, I felt I wouldn't until I gave her this last loving gbit of submission.

"Miss O., please let me come."

"Yes..." Octavia squealed.

"Go ahead and come, sweetheart, let it all out," she added, working her left hand under me while grabbing my cock at the root with her right. "Ten wonderful nights."

I began to come the second Octavia pulled her hand ever so slightly up my shaft. Pushing her fingers deeper into my ass, getting me to all but quake, the first shot landed on the girl's right breast, then Octavia leaned down and took the rest of my hot thick load full in her face.

I bucked, whimpered, shook, and spurted. So much came across the woman's pretty pale face, across her eyes, into her mouth as she held her lips open to take what she could and more down her chin. I had never been one of those guys who felt a blow-job — even the few times that I did come from one — incomplete unless a woman swallowed my come, nor did I have a genuine interest in blowing across a woman's face. But as I reported, here was a woman who had jerked me off into her mouth on more than one occasion, and I must admit, right then, finally being able to release after being caged by Octavia, it did indeed feel good to drench her like that.

* * * * *

There came a marketable shift in our relationship about two months after my visit when Octavia caged me. We hadn't been in each other's presence since, and more time seemed to stretch between our phone calls, texts, and emails. When we did talk, we didn't engage in any truly naughty communication, although we still gave great phone.

There was just something strained, and we never again talked much about anything kinky as we did just coax each other to masturbate by imagining we were lying together. I sensed what it was coming down to was that I was skirting the question of if it was feasible for Octavia to move to me or me to her. While the woman had enjoyed her freedom since her last steady girlfriend and generally liked to do as she pleased unencumbered by monogamy, Octavia had made it plain that she could be just as happy settling in, down, under, and over with the right person. But I was nobody's Mr. Right — more like Mr. Right Now — even though, as I admit above, I sensed Octavia, and I could have made a solid couple, and my heart was leading that way.

Per my usual, without consciously meaning to, I started to back away from yet another relationship that probably would have been fantastic. The mature, smart, sexy, and together lady realized there was no way to take what we had any further, and despite how hot we could get one another, her emotions cooled via my complacency. Soon we weren't even managing the requisite weekly phone call, and then we stopped talking together.

God knows what the hell I was trying to hold onto or hold out for. I had never met a woman as kinky as Octavia, and I knew she could have consistently delivered what I needed as I could have for her in all ways. Tragic figure or immature boy-man, I'll leave it for you to decide, if you even care to, but I found myself yet again running to the end with another woman.

Brat Pays

By William D. Prystauk

I'm a brat.

In the world of kink, that means I'm a real pain in the ass to the one who dominates me because I love to push buttons, push boundaries, and push-push-push to gain attention.

Well, today was the day where my darling Black Rose had enough and she stepped up her game to keep me in check. After all, during a punishment session where she whipped me with a lame flogger as if it had been made of felt, I laughed. Not at her so much as the pathetic toy, but it's never good to make a dominant partner feel like they can't deliver.

Now, vanilla guests were coming over for a quick midday visit, which was strange to me, and I wasn't allowed to be part of the party or whatever my Mistress, Ms. Rose had planned.

Before the guests' arrival, my Black Rose brought me by the cock to the edge of the bed we shared in her red passion bedroom with black-and-white furniture and pink accents. Part of the pink accents was the comforter on the queen bed.

"No party fun for me, Ms. Rose?"

"Not with the way you've been acting."

Her face seemed more taut than usual and with the pained look in her eye, I realize that my earlier remark had shaken her performance confidence. "On your stomach and don't rub your dick."

"Can I at least rub yours, Ms. Rose?"

"Get on the goddamn bed, bitch!"

She wasn't joking.

Black Rose was her name, not just because of her beautiful skin and the pink rose she often wore above her left ear that stood out from her long black mane, but because of the rose tattoo on her gorgeous little ass. Her thin frame and flat chest sported no hair, and she had shaved away the tuft from her cock eons ago. But ordering me down to the bed got me even harder and I hoped she'd shove her sleek cock down my throat.

I got face down on the bed and didn't move though my hard-on begged to glide across the smooth comforter.

"I'd better not see your hips move an inch."

"Yes, Mistress Rose."

"Hands behind your back and don't move."

I did so and Black Rose went off to get whatever she needed to keep me trussed up while she and whoever else were drinking and laughing and enjoying a regular good time. Some of her equipment hit the comforter. Instinctively, I turned my head to see what I was in for.

"I said don't fucking move!"

With that, she pounced and secured black wrist cuffs on me with a metal clip holding them together.

I heard her breathe out because Ms. Rose was thrilled to have my hands bound without me trying to wriggle away from her. She moved quickly, securing cuffs on my upper arms held together by a metal bar. Now, I knew she meant business because this was no longer "fun bondage time" and things were getting uncomfortable. I had been too much of a brat and needed to apologize but I couldn't do so without asking permission first.

"Mistress Rose, can I please ask you something?"

She paused for a second, maybe because I was being so nice — even submissive instead of bratty. "Keep your damned mouth shut. I've... I've really fucking had it with you."

I had clearly disappointed my sweet Black Rose. Sometimes, I push too far in order to get her to make me suffer a little more because she's often too sweet when I don't want her to be. Now, I had no doubt I'd feel deeper repercussions sooner and in a harsher manner.

Since I could only roll over at this point, and to prevent me from saying something smart, she stood before me. I peered up as best I could and she let me look. Wearing a soft red sweater and leather skirt, she slipped off the pink undies that trapped her cock.

Black Rose folded the panties she'd worn all morning and then said, "Pick up your head and open your mouth."

The look on her face told me I shouldn't fuck around. "Can I suck you off, Ms. Rose?"

She gritted her teeth and shoved the underwear into my mouth.

Though she was pissed, I saw the hard bulge under her skirt. Then came the rip of tape off its roll. When she got the tape onto my mouth, I heard her sigh again.

"I swear to God. You cannot make any noise. Nothing. We'll be right downstairs. If someone says they think they heard something, I'll put a cage on your dick for a week and edge the Hell out of you."

The last thing I wanted was chastity or to have her jerk me off or suck me off to the point of climax only to stop, wait a while, and then start again. Maybe she really didn't want me to fuck up because after the tape, she tied a tight black bandana over my mouth.

"The best slave is a gagged slave."

I nodded. But maybe she should have said, "The best slave is a well-behaved slave," because that I wasn't. And with the binding and gagging and knowing how her delicious cock was mere inches from me, I couldn't help but slowly drive my hard-on into the comforter.

"You goddamn bitch!"

Her anger wasn't just about me rubbing my penis when I wasn't allowed to, she really didn't want me staining that pink comforter with a drop of pre cum.

She grasped something I couldn't see while lifting my bound hands. With the pressure on my shoulders because of my elevated arms, my face pressed hard into the comforter and I couldn't move. A flurry of thick rubber tendrils from her whip came hard and fast onto my ass. The sting radiated throughout my body and the best I could do was scream through the layered gags.

"Shut the fuck up and take it, you pussy!"

The rubber came down sharper along my ass and the back of my legs. I imagined her lifting her arm as high as possible to drive those many strips onto my flesh. Sweat consumed me, my shoulders ached, taking a breath proved difficult, and my muffled screams fell into the short sounds of sobbing.

Finally, she released my hands that fell just above my red-hot ass. Her hands rolled me over onto my back.

"Cry all you want. It's your fault."

I was pissed and did my best to not fall into a full-blown fit of crying but my ass burned, and with each beat of my heart, I felt the pain pulse through my fiery cheeks.

Ms. Rose grabbed other things now: A leather sheath for the shaft of my cock and a ball-splitter harness that would also enwrap the base of my penis in a ring. The purpose of the sheath was to make certain that if I tried to rub my dick, nothing would happen because I'd be devoid of sensation. Plus, if I pressed my dick into the bed, my suddenly firm balls would feel it too, causing a ton of pain.

When finished, Black Rose strangled my cock with her hand — and bit down hard on its head as looked right at me.

The pain was so excruciating I thought I'd piss in her mouth.

"How'd that feel? Good, bitch?"

My eyes were wet. I saw stars and looked down to make sure she hadn't bitten off the tip. I gave her the right answer and nodded.

"Aww," she mocked, "you're bein' good now, ain't cha?" I nodded again as I fought off pain everywhere. "Well, things come in threes, right?"

My eyes were shut and wet and I took in deep air as if that would somehow drive the throbbing pain away and make her teeth marks vanish from my cock. "Whip... One bite of your dick... I know what else you need."

Mistress Rose took her top off and laid it on her pillow. Then her skirt came off. But she kept the stockings and garters on her firm legs, along with her little boots.

Her dick was hard and jumping a little from her taking charge of me for real this time. That's when she rolled me back onto my stomach. I heard the cap pop on the lube. I heard her rub her cock down and then wipe off her hands.

"Spread your legs like the little cunt you are."

I did so. But I wasn't in the mood for anal and that was definitely my problem, not hers. Ms. Rose wasn't big but she knew how to fuck me hard and make it hurt in the process, if she wanted that to happen — and I had no doubt she did. And since I'd been an asshole, there'd be no anal foreplay to relax the muscles of my anus. But I willed myself to relax my ass as she rammed her dick into me right up to the hilt.

Laying on top of me, she put her hand over my mouth as if I hadn't been gagged at all and drove her dick in and out of me, giving an extra squeeze of the hips like a little exclamation point. I grunted as my body moved with each of her painful thrusts.

She panted in my ear as I mewed and cried, and I'd only here her whisper "Fuck" once in a while.

With guests on the way and knowing she had bested me like the strong Dom I knew she could be, Black Rose gripped me tighter still as she shot her load deep inside me.

"Fuck... fucking goddammit... I'm filling your ass with cum."

I conjured up an extra loud groan as a thank you. She grunted and kept on pumping, doing her damnedest to squeeze out every drop into me.

When finished, she breathed as if just finishing a marathon. Without saying anything, I heard more noise and more lube as I tried to hold myself together. Tried to breathe. Tried to relax an asshole that had been violated and fucked until raw. From the sounds behind me, I knew what was coming. I buried my face into the comforter and begged with a series of noises that would get me nowhere but maybe get my Mistress off again.

"Oh," Ms. Rose said from behind, "let me show you what your little bitch self is gonna get."

She came round in front of me and stood with a smile. Ms. Rose held a lubed black dildo attached to a harness in her hand. I really mewed now.

"Yeah, it's bigger than me. More girth too. Think of it as me hugging you from the inside and not letting go."

Ms. Rose didn't ram it into my sore asshole, she pressed the tip of it against my anal lips and slowly inserted the dildo up to that edge where the hood of the head came to an end before the shaft, and then she drew it back before doing it all over again.

The more I moaned, getting louder as that head spread me open wider, the more she hummed — and giggled. "Look at your boi pussy open up for me. It wants dick bad."

With that, she finally drove the fake dick into me a half-inch at a time. "Your ass is so sucking this in. Such a good lil brat."

Once this monster filled me to the point where I had to find a new way to breathe, Black Rose calmly secured the straps of the harness around my waist and thighs to hold the dildo in place.

"Now there's no way for you to shit it out."

I couldn't. Although exhausted, even if I tried, that dildo wasn't going anywhere.

Mistress Black Rose then bound my feet and tightened a strap above my knees.

My ass hurt in too many places. I felt the relentless pressure from the dildo. My balls ached. My cock hurt. And trying not to moan and groan seemed impossible.

Black Rose flipped me on my back. She looked down at me like a panther who knew she'd won. She lit a cigarette and blew smoke to the ceiling as she toyed with my hard on.

"Two hours. You have to hold on for two hours." She inhaled and hummed again as she did so. "Let your asshole relax because that dildo ain't going nowhere."

Tears mixed with sweat and I knew my face must be red.

I shut my eyes and writhed and hummed and tried to find some semblance of comfort, which was impossible. When I opened my eyes, I saw my Mistress recording my suffering from her phone.

"That's it," she sang. "Smile for me, baby fuck."

Ms. Rose put down the phone, took a last hit from the cigarette before putting it out, and she laid on the bed with me. As I struggled and mewed, she told me to, "Shh…" and rocked me as she held me.

"Hey, look at me," she said with a tap to my cheek. I looked at her. "I'm going to hurt you more later, okay?"

I nodded.

She shut her eyes and kissed my forehead. When she pulled back to look at me, her eyes sparkled.

As I resorted to heavy breathing to avoid grunts and groans, my Mistress ignored me as she enjoyed another cigarette and got ready. She even touched up her makeup and put on a fresh pair of panties.

Then the moment came: The doorbell rang.

Mistress made a pouty face and kissed my gag. She gave me a little wave and said, "Love you" as she left and closed the door.

I love you too, Mistress Rose, I thought. I love you so damn much.

THEMES: camming, cuckolding, dominance/submission, emotional affair, exhibitionism, humiliation, master/slave. Oral sex, piercings, piv sex, sloppy seconds, voyeurism

The Master

By Liam Herne

A regular housewife bored with her routine, Gigi joined the Camfuze community, an adult site and a fun way to further explore other people and sex. At first, Gigi only watched. She watched hands on anonymous cocks stroking. She watched girls touch themselves and fuck themselves with dildos. She watched men in women's lingerie. She watched men overpower their female partners, sometimes tying them or gagging them or merely manipulating their erogenous zones until the women writhed.

Some of what she saw, she incorporated into her own bedroom. Her husband, Ernie, loved it. Over time, Gigi thought it may be even more fun to open her own room on the site. Ernie agreed, because based on what he'd experienced so far, he wouldn't have anything to lose.

The positive responses Gigi got when she first opened her room felt somewhat overwhelming but good. It uplifted her. When she mentioned this to Ernie, he said that she had found her sanctuary. He liked the changes in her confidence. He liked her new comfort in her skin.

Camfuze had given her a place to escape to, a place to be her inner self without being judged as she had always been by family and friends. Or at the very least scrutinized to the point of making her feel inadequate and uncomfortable. None of that was present on Camfuze and it indeed became a sanctuary.

Everyone was there to have fun. To be friendly and hopefully make some friends but not to get involved with anyone. Gigi believed she had a good and happy relationship going with Ernie.

After being on Camfuze for a time, one of Gigi's regulars started catching her attention. BruteGrendel. He carried out intelligent conversations, immediately recognized Gigi's tattoo (surprising for an obscure literary reference, but then look at his handle) which pleased her immensely. He possessed an assertiveness that grabbed the attention of everyone in the room. He didn't come off desperate and horny, like most of her admirers. Those desperate, horny men jerking off and voicing their encouragement while looking at Gigi's images would remain quiet when he said something, anything.

Even though Gigi would not admit it to anyone, not even herself, her heart rate quickened when his name lit up in her room. She rationalized her reaction as a response to someone strong and intelligent who kept her entertained. Nothing more.

Days turned into weeks. The open room conversations with Grendel, this magnetic man, progressed to private messaging and eventually to private cam-to-cam meetings. Gigi had not intentionally planned this, nor did she actually want to get more involved with a person on Camfuze. BruteGrendel had a presence about him that was alluring and undeniable that kept her coming back to him like a moth drawn to light.

As a good wife, Gigi mentioned that there was a follower in her room that was becoming particularly chummy. Yet, she could not fully open up to Ernie on what was taking place inside her. Her faithfulness to Ernie and the desire to be good to him felt like it was being challenged. Not aggressively challenged, but enough for the anxiety of Gigi's emotions to come into play. Despite the inner conflict, Gigi felt powerlessness to walk away from this new friend. Even an unwillingness, and that unwillingness shocked her.

After some soul searching, Gigi conceded her weakness stemmed from Grendel's strength. He exuded a dominance that was holding her captive. And Ernie would not understand. Ernie would like to believe that he had strength and presence, too. He had been the one to care for Gigi when life proved difficult. How could she explain that she connected with this stranger on some animalistic level? What would Ernie think if he knew he might have competition roaming in his territory? So Gigi did not elaborate on chummy.

Yet, cam-to-cam meetings had the effect of slowly lowering Gigi's resistance to the new friend. When BruteGrendel opened his cam to her for the first time, he asked her to remove the robe she had on. As Gigi stood there naked for him, he undressed himself. Gigi's heart fluttered and her stomach flipped at the sight of Grendel's naked body and meaty cock, even flaccid. Together, nude, the experience felt like a dream — real because the technology made it real, but somehow still safe and unreal because Grendel wasn't really there with Gigi. But it felt like he was. It felt, to Gigi, that is she wanted to reach out and touch him, she could. And he could reach out and touch her.

Each time Gigi met on cam with BruteGrendel his hold became stronger. Gigi met his every request. When Gigi masturbated with a dildo, he repeatedly told her it was his cock fucking her. Those words drove her towards climax. But he didn't let her cum. He denied her climax, forcing her to watch his cock get harder, thicker and longer while his hand closed around it and he masturbated, slowly, studying Gigi as she stood transfixed by him.

Her ability to hold back her climax became difficult, more so with each passing meeting. When he, thankfully, gave Gigi permission to climax, she erupted in a full body climax as thick, white streams of his seed gushed from the head of his cock, a pulsing volcano that continued to erupt, powerful and unceasing. Gigi had never seen that much response from a man, never seen that much fluid.

Gigi clamped tight on the dildo, imagining that her pussy had locked around BruteGrendel's volcanic cock, milking him and letting him fill her with his seed.

Each meeting brought a pang of guilt. Not for camming with BruteGrendel, that much Ernie knew, but for the uncontrollable bodily responses and the feelings that Gigi had developed for BruteGrendel. The depth of the lust, the blinding power of the need. And Gigi couldn't deny her emotions, or block them, or control them. This caused Gigi anxiety, parts of her wanted to resist. She wanted to be true to Ernie.

She carried condoms with her. She never intended to need them, but somehow it seemed less unfaithful if another man didn't come inside her. If he didn't really touch her. Because at this point, she had learned that planting seed in a pussy dictated ownership, the marking of territory so to speak. But that did not stop Gigi from fantasizing about BruteGrendel filling her. His thick cock stretching her tight pussy, his abundant seed gushing through her. There was nothing wrong with fantasizing, right? But Gigi never mentioned this to Ernie just in case it would not sit well with him.

The meetings on cam with BruteGrendel became more regular. Gigi anticipated them. Her emotions had developed into an obsession, creating a need to see and be with him. Yet the guilt never subsided. The feeling of being torn between two men became a daily struggle. She started comparing Ernie's cock with that of BruteGrendel. Not that one could compare.

BruteGrendel had a thicker, longer and harder cock than Ernie. Even flaccid, Grendel's cock hung prouder. That in itself was not a big deal, but it did make Gigi wonder what effect that huge cock could have. She masturbated with the dildo, slender and short, and thought about Ernie. She wondered if that was even fair. The dildo might be harder than Ernie.

Over the weeks that followed, BruteGrendel's control over Gigi tightened and reached deeper. Gigi's desire to please him became stronger. She masturbated freely on his commands, anyway he wanted. Anywhere he wanted. Whether he wanted Gigi to penetrate puss or her ass or both, she complied. BruteGrendel pushed Gigi further under his spell by asking whose pussy or ass she was fucking. Automatically, Gigi heard her voice say, "Yours, Grendel, they belong to you."

Each time the cam sessions ended guilt washed over Gigi, as really she belonged to Ernie. She should belong to Ernie, body and soul. But when Gigi was with BruteGrendel, she could not help or stop herself. Gigi's emotional infidelity could only be excused by the fact that she had never slept with BruteGrendel. What happened in her head and when she was alone couldn't really count if no other man had even cum inside her.

But then BruteGrendel wanted to meet. It was inevitable. He asked for a place and a time to meet Gigi. And he made it perfectly clear that this wasn't purely a meeting. Electricity filled Gigi when she heard that request. A mixture of fear and excitement fluttered through her stomach. She heard a voice reply to him, a voice she later recognized as her own, to agree that it may be time to meet in person.

BruteGrendel noticed Gigi's nervousness and reassured her that not only was it time to meet, but that it was the "right" thing for her and him to do. Hearing the word "right" made Gigi clench her thighs together. Her juices flooded her panties and an excitement she had never felt before flowed from her breasts deep into her abdomen. What was happening to her? Gigi asked herself. Why could she not keep in control when in BruteGrendel's presence?

Later that evening, Gigi approached Ernie about BruteGrendel's request. At first, Ernie seemed flummoxed as he had no idea how serious it had gotten. He attributed some of the recent bedroom activities to his own prowess and not Gigi's increased interest. So, she played it off. She said something about BruteGrendel that seemed different, interesting. She was curious and wanted to explore it.

That's what she told herself, too. It was just for fun. Gigi wanted to forget all those conflicting feelings and come home to Ernie afterwards with as much love for him as before she left. Get the lust out of her system and grow up. Be the adult in the room.

Ernie didn't seem sold on the idea, and Gigi thought she saw some hurt in his eyes. He asked questions, mostly about her safety. As he pondered, Gigi stroked his hand. He slowly nodded. Gigi broached the next topic.

Grendel wanted her to spend the night.

Ernie refused. A couple hours, that was one thing, but a night was out of the question. She pointed out that it was far, and it would be late and dark and she would be tired. Perhaps it would be better for all of them if she stayed. Ernie insisted on a hotel. Nothing too personal. Something neutral. Gigi agreed. And he was to know exactly where she was, and wanted text messages to assure him that she was safe. Again she agreed. After humming and harring for a bit, Ernie reluctantly gave his assent.

But he gave her two conditions: ANY man with her must use a condom and NO man other than him must ever finish inside her. Gigi agreed. The look in his eyes told her he would not negotiate.

When Gigi gave BruteGrendel the news, he gave that self-assured look that she loved so much and smiled that sly, plotting smile. Gigi blushed and grinned, unable to help either reaction.

Gigi arrived at the place Grendel had selected, with Ernie's blessing. The evening would start at a pub and end at the hotel. In person, his presence carried even stronger than on screen. The quiet confidence he had didn't obtrude into the room but within his proximity it was undeniable. They had supper, a light meal as neither really cared about food, but the pub had good music and BruteGrendel suggested staying to listen and share drinks.

She wanted drinks. It would settle her nerves. But at the same time, alcohol would render her not exactly herself. Compromise her decision making skills. Ernie would want her stone cold sober. She had to drink smartly. BruteGrendel had yet to earn her trust.

The hotel stood across the street. BruteGrendel had booked a room with a jacuzzi. The bedroom had a king-size bed. The jacuzzi had been filled and Gigi could feel the heat from the water and hear the bubbling from the jets. There was champagne on ice and Gigi muttered a low moan of enthusiasm.

"You are worth all of this and much, much more."

BruteGrendel swirled his arms around Gigi and kissed her hard and long. His mouth consuming hers and his tongue plunging into her in a way that she could only describe as mimicking what he'd like to do with his cock inside her. Instinctively, Gigi wanted to pull back, to ask him to slow down. Her body betrayed her. Her knees buckled and her head fogged. She swooned under the hard, urgent kiss. If it weren't for his grasp, Gigi would have fallen. Gigi was dead weight against him. When BruteGrendel released her lips, Gigi gasped for air. With a smug look and an air of satisfaction, he moved to the bathroom and motioned for Gigi to follow.

"Undress me," he commanded.

He stood in front of the jacuzzi. Gigi, fingers trembling, reached out to unbutton his shirt. She started at the bottom, taking the time to inhale and calm her nerves. Except when she did, his aroma entered her nostrils and quickened the beat of her heart. She closed her eyes.

"Look at me," BruteGrendel said.

She opened her eyes. She placed her fingers on the next button.

"Look me in the eye," he said.

She did. It seemed like ages until she finished buttoning. She pushed the shirt off his shoulders, chased it down his arms. Gigi savored the feel of his body. She peeled up his undershirt. He raised his arms and she brought the shirt over his head. Regaining her confidence she unfastened his pants, cupped his ass as she encouraged the pants to fall over his hips. The pants shimmied down his thighs. Her hands didn't move, firmly against his ass.

Grendel sunk one hand into her hair, pulling her head back.

"Aren't we getting bold"

His firmness of hold scared her, but at the same time, puss was dripping from the whole series of events. She loosened her grip. He chuckled.

"It's okay," he said. "I like it."

He released her hair. She slid his underpants down and released his cock. He stood there, boldly. She crouched and removed Grendel's socks one at a time. As Gigi rose to her feet, her eyes roamed. Everything about him seemed bigger in real life. Even flaccid, she marveled at his meaty cock. Gigi flashed a nervous smile and he returned it with an expression of unwavering confidence. He stepped into the jacuzzi.

"Go pour the champagne," he commanded. "And when you come back, you'd better be naked."

Shaking uncontrollably, Gigi shed her clothes in the bedroom, poured the champagne and took a moment to breathe, wondering if those were butterflies or dinosaurs in her stomach. She walked into the bathroom. His eyes devoured her. Grendel's eyes stared and consumed every inch of her, yet she had never felt less exposed.

"I have seen you so many times," he said, "but you are more beautiful than I thought possible."

She smiled, a self-assured, happy smile.

"Nothing is going to stop me from owning you," he said softly but without a hint of doubt.

Then, as Gigi stood there frozen, he said, "Come in."

Gigi lowered herself into the warm bubbling water. She went toward him to hand him his champagne. He took the glass and with his free hand pulled her onto his lap facing him. Gigi straddled him and sat in his lap. Gigi could feel his soft yet thick cock against her stomach. That was how they drank champagne, flesh close and surrounded by water. BruteGrendel took the empty glasses and put them on a ledge behind him. He pulled Gigi closer, their bodies closing tightly against each other.

BruteGrendel kissed her deeply as his hands went across her back and downwards. He filled his hands with the cheeks of Gigi's ass. Already Gigi could not restrain the noises coming from her throat. BruteGrendel lifted her just enough to allow his cock to fall forward. Then he lowered Gigi against it. His hands slipped up her back again. The entire time BruteGrendel never stopped kissing her.

The kisses progressed. He started with her lips, covered her face, then neck. He explored her breasts, her nipples, her multiple piercings and the metal shapes that filled them. He kissed and suckled them all. With every affection, his cock grew stronger and harder beneath her pussy as Gigi straddled the shaft.

As he hardened, BruteGrendel shifted against her, rocking slightly to engage his shaft against puss's lips. Gigi couldn't help but lean into the motion and she felt puss's lips flaying open and surrounding his expanding erection. This exposed Gigi's clit. The pressure and movement from riding him so smoothly made her want to be taken, and it was building quickly. The size of his cock beneath her thighs was more than ready to take her. As if reading her mind, Grendel pushed the bulbous head of his cock against her entrance.

Panic seized her like a strike of lightning. She had left the condoms with her clothes in the bedroom but she had no will left. She couldn't break away now. It seemed impossible to leave him and retreat to the bedroom for the condoms. One of the rules would be broken and Gigi had no desire to stop it.

The pressure of BruteGrendel's cock head pushed into her, stretching puss and filling puss unlike anything she had ever felt before. His thick shaft worked into her, probably only three-quarters of the way in, and already deeper than Ernie could ever fill her. Gigi gasped, torn between bliss and discomfort, because she couldn't quite label the sensation. She just knew she didn't want it to stop. And then Gigi managed to say it. In the meekest voice she had ever heard herself use: "Please... don't cum... inside... me."

Gigi already violated one rule. It would be nice if BruteGrendel could respect the final rule.

And sure... Gigi understood. She belonged to Ernie. She had pledged herself to Ernie. She had borne his children. He was the head of their unit, their clan. She had to respect him. A voice whispered inside her head asking what he had done to earn and keep that respect? If she were here, in another man's arms, another man's cock deep inside her didn't that say something?

BruteGrendel had not replied. Instead, he lifted Gigi out of the water, his cock still impaling her, and carried her into the bedroom. Bodies still engaged and dripping wet, he fell with Gigi onto the bed. She let out a cry as his body covered hers. He felt so good. Any doubt she had disintegrated. BruteGrendel kissed her, pulled her arms up and pinned her wrists above her head. And then he plowed into her, again and again, roughly, with abandon, groins slamming together. Gigi's body responded with gusto, juices weeping from her body, surrounding his massive cock, allowing him to thrust deeper and deeper into her pussy.

The sloppy sex noises surrounded them, the wet, sucking sounds of her pussy, his balls slapping against her ass. The complete length of his thick, meaty shaft disappeared into puss when he plowed forward. The thickness and length of his cock filling Gigi blinded her with new highs of lust. Her body offered a tremble. Sensing it, BruteGrendel groaned and retreated. Gigi opened her mouth to protest. He set his finger against her lips.

BruteGrendel spun her onto her hands and knees. Forcefully, he rammed into Gigi from behind sending shivers through puss. Hard and without any thought of mercy, he pounded into Gigi over and over and over again. He took a handful of hair and pulled her head backwards as he rode her. She moaned. With his free hand, he smacked the cheeks of her ass.

"Why did you ask me that?" he said, a strange tinge in his voice. "Why did you ask me not to cum inside you?"

He continued spanking her. Tears rolled down her face. She tried to explain, between the bouts of torment from his bludgeoning cock and his stinging hands. He fucked Gigi harder. She summarized Ernie's requests. Grendel yanked her hair harder, hit the cheeks of her ass harder. Her cheeks glowed blood red and were hot to the touch, but there was no pain anymore. Only pleasure as he continued hitting her ass and pounding her pussy with his cock.

Without warning, he pulled from her again and flung her onto her back. He placed her legs over his shoulders, cock rubbing up against Gigi's amazingly wet dripping puss. She had never felt it gush like this. With one quick thrust he sank thoroughly into her. The depth and the angle of his penetration skewered her. His face came very close to Gigi's.

Through low growls, BruteGrendel told her that Ernie was not strong enough to own her. That he, BruteGrendel, owned her and would dominate her.

"I will be your Dom," he said.

Only a fire and brimstone preacher could have sounded more ominous and authoritative.

"He can't stop me," BruteGrendel said as he fucked Gigi, his cock thrusting into the base of her womb. "When I am done with you, and I am nowhere near done with you, you will realize how weak he is. His cock won't satisfy you again. His seed will do nothing for you."

BruteGrendel repeated this, over and over, still pounding puss mercilessly demanding that Gigi look him in the eyes as his words rang in her ears causing her pussy to ache for release. Then he made her say it. That he was her Dom. That he owned her. That Ernie was nothing. That Ernie could never please her again.

The sucking sounds continued from Gigi's pussy. Both her groin and his wore the white evidence of her arousal. BruteGrendel grunted more fiercely as his climax approached. The heat of his body, his strength and dominance engulfed her. Gigi's hips worked with his. He released her legs and grabbed her shoulders enabling him to pull even deeper into her. Gigi's legs closed around his back and her heels dug into the cheeks of his butt. Loud rasping sounds came from her throat as she clung to him.

With a succession of wild roars and frantic thrusts, BruteGrendel released into Gigi, a warm explosion of seed, as the fervor of orgasm consumed both of them. The little faithfulness that remained for Ernie silently screamed "no, no, no" as thick streams of Grendel's cum floated into her womb.

His ownership continued throughout the night, so forceful that eventually Gigi's loyalty broke. She no longer felt Ernie deserved to own her. She could not imagine his cock ever satisfying her again. And the thought of Ernie's seed in BruteGrendel's pussy was unimaginable. But even so, Gigi still loved Ernie. It was a different kind of love and one that still needed to be defined. BruteGrendel, as her Dom, would end up defining that love in time.

Gigi arrived home later than Ernie expected. He noticed a different air about her. She was cordial enough yet emotionally distant. The hug and kiss were brief, the kind of hug and kiss reserved for a distant relative met for the first time. He asked if everything went okay. Gigi stood quietly for a bit as if collecting her thoughts. She motioned to him to come sit on the couch.

"I have something to tell you," she said.

Gigi started off by admitting she was not totally honest about BruteGrendel. She spoke to him in private messaging more than she let on. And when she started going private cam-to-cam with him she did it more often than she said. And when she said it was just for fun, well eventually it turned to more than fun. Emotional feelings started creeping in.

Ernie asked why she did not tell him that when it first started happening. Gigi sighed and said she thought about it but couldn't. She did not want to hurt him but she didn't want to lose what was developing with BruteGrendel.

"But what was the big deal in losing this friend," Ernie said. "You have many friends on Camfuze."

"There was something… magnetic about him," Gigi said. "I could not fully understand it till we met in person, until what happened last night."

Ernie asked what happened. Gigi had no rehearsed speech so she said what came to mind.

"He is a Dom," Gigi said looking her partner in the eyes, "a very, very strong Dom." "A true Dom."

"And although at the time I did not think of him as that, it was clearly his strength as a Dom that made our relationship grow as it did."

Gigi kept talking.

"And without me knowing it, he wanted to make me his, to own me."

Gigi paused.

"And what I thought was going to be just a fun meeting with him last night turned out to be something more."

"What do you mean?" Ernie asked.

There was no other way to delay. Gigi needed to tell him. She looked away so as not to see the hurt in his eyes.

"He owned me last night. He made me his."

"But how was that possible?" Ernie stammered. "You're mine."

"I tried to resist," Gigi replied. "Believe me I tried, but his dominance was just too strong. I folded. Yes, I folded under his strength. I know now I am a submissive and a submissive can't fight against such dominance!"

Gigi was almost crying by now. Crying because part of her felt bad for Ernie and part of her was angry at him. Gigi got her composure back and said even though she was now owned by another he was the father of their children and as such she loved him for that. She quickly added the love she felt for him now was not the same love she felt for him yesterday but promised to be honest with him from now on. She could not describe how she felt but he had to know it was different. And they could work through this and make this new arrangement work but if he felt he couldn't he was free to leave without any bad feelings.

With a sullen look, Ernie said he can't leave. Even though she couldn't love him the way he loved her anymore, he couldn't leave. He needed her. One of the predictions BruteGrendel made about Ernie had come true. Could it be true what BruteGrendel had said about Ernie?

"If you are going to stay you have to accept things are going to be different. And my Dom wants you to see that difference first hand and how it all started."

Gigi opened her laptop and placed it on the table and played the recording BruteGrendel had insisted on. Ernie saw Gigi lying naked on a bed. The camera was positioned so that Ernie had a bird's eye view. Into focus came BruteGrendel and went and laid naked next to Gigi. Ernie witnessed her kissing Grendel with passion. Running her hands across his body to his thick cock. Masturbating him while she continued kissing him. She moved down his body kissing his chest, his nipples, working down his stomach to his cock. Closing her mouth around his cock, Gigi sucked deep and long and Ernie saw the Dom's cock became harder and thicker. Ernie's eyes were fixed on the laptop.

"You like what you see so far, don't you?" Gigi said.

Ernie mumbled something unintelligible but continued looking. The size of the Dom's cock made Ernie feel instantly inadequate and unworthy. Why he felt this unworthiness he had no idea but he did. Ernie saw BruteGrendel upend Gigi onto her back and without a condom, he forced his thick, meaty cock into her.

Gigi told Ernie to remove his cock from his pants. She wanted to see if his sissy dick was getting hard. Reluctantly Ernie took out his cock. It was indeed getting harder. Gigi encouraged him to masturbate while watching the recording. Ernie could not deny it. He was getting turned on by watching BruteGrendel with his thick long cock fucking Gigi without a condom!

Ernie watched every stroke BruteGrendel made into Gigi. Watching as Gigi's pussy coated Grendel's thick shaft with creamy wetness allowing it to go deeper until the whole length of his shaft was inside and his balls were banging up against Gigi's ass.

Ernie had not noticed that Gigi had pulled off her panties exposing her well-used cunt. He was transfixed on the screen watching Gigi and her Dom while masturbating at the same time.

"That's right, watch my Dom fucking me with his strong cock while you masturbate your weak cock," Gigi said.

Those words did not sting Ernie but were uncomfortable for him to hear for the first time. He could not deny it to himself that he was turned on by watching the recording.

"That's right, jerk off that small cock of yours," Gigi said.

"Watch how my Dom fucks me with his huge cock."

"You can see how I'm loving it."

"You can see why you can't fuck me anymore."

"Your dick will never satisfy me again."

Ernie stood there masturbating his inadequate cock faster and faster.

"Now you don't cum 'til the good part. I want you to save it for when Sir cums inside me."

Gigi played with her clit. Ernie enjoyed everything about the scene.

Ernie watched as Grendel jerked spasmodically and puss clenched tight.

"That's Sir cumming inside His pussy. Filling me with his hot thick seed. And puss is feeding hungrily on it."

Ernie could not hold back anymore. Gigi told him to shoot his weak seed on the floor while he watched puss feed on Sir's strong seed. Ernie's seed dribbled onto the floor and Gigi felt a wicked satisfaction. He, then, for the first time, noticed Gigi's exposed pussy and how messy it was. Gigi told Ernie that Sir wanted Ernie to see how well it had been used and then to clean His pussy.

"Now be a good boy and go fetch a damp wet cloth."

He returned with the damp cloth.

"Sir first wants you to use your tongue to clean His pussy," she said.

Obediently Ernie dropped between Gigi's legs and started licking her pussy.

"Taste our cum and clean pussy nicely."

She stood unwavering as he worked.

"Sir was right about you, you are a pussy boy. But you know I still love you, don't you?"

As she ran her fingers through his hair, she asked him to wipe her with the cloth.

"And from now on you will be known as 'PB,' my pussy boy." Even a submissive needs her toys right? she thought to herself.

She smiled warmly, like the devoted wife and mother she used to be. He finished cleaning her. Gigi said to no one in particular that she thought she might enjoy this new found darkness that Sir had introduced her to as she watched Ernie shuffle out the room to the bathroom with the cloth.

THEMES: age gap, ass play, cock worship, cuckolding, exhibitionism, oral sex, piv sex, sloppy seconds, voyeurism

Mia and the Dance

By Angie Ravenstone

Mia had told George to meet her at Mr. V.'s house. She wasn't sure exactly why she did it, but she supposed it was because Mr. V made her feel comfortable and empowered but also safe — George wouldn't do anything she didn't want him to do if Mr. V introduced himself, or that's what she liked to believe.

She bought a sleeveless little black dress for the dance. Formfitting and hugging her waist. Simple stockings and plain black shoes. And a red scarf. She thought the red scarf was sophisticated.

She found a bunch of candy in her purse and sat at Mr. V's table sharing sweets with him while he made coffee. She pulled a packet of pop rocks from the bottom of her bag. She poured some into her mouth and kissed Mr. V while they exploded. He chuckled, regained his composure, and suggested she try that again on his cock.

Immediately, she fell to her knees and greedily worked his cock from his pants. It swelled in her hands as she released it. With eagerness, she filled her mouth with candy and slurped her way down his cock. She licked and sucked and explored with quickness, wanting to catch the reaction of the candy in full depth. And then he was sticky and sweet so she consumed him trying to whip away the flavor. He moaned and grabbed her hair, gently guiding her at first, but soon rougher and with more need as he growled and moaned. And then he warned her — that he was close, and she devoured and sucked and swallowed until he whimpered and told her to stop. Then she delicately pulled away, licking the head oh so softly.

The playful look in her eye and her sticky lips prompted Mr. V to kiss her and reach for her breasts, squeezing them through the bodice of the dress. Her enthusiastic responses got him hard again. And he folded her over the table like he had at least a dozen times before, pulled down her stockings and black lace panties and slammed into her dripping pussy as he pulled her by the hips against his aching cock. Her tight, hot cunt electrified his cock. He pounded her. Despite her youth, she mewed in delight, screaming for him the harder he drove into her. She twitched around him, her eagerness to please leaving her prone to cum at the slightest touch. And he filled that pussy with his seed.

Before he withdrew, her panting against the table, he pulled a fairly good sized jeweled anal plug from his pocket. He fingered her wet pussy and swollen clit with his free hand and lubricated the plug with their juices. Then, he let his cock fall from her and worked his finger and then the plug into her ass.

"To remind you of me," Mr. V. said.

Mia reassembled her clothes just in time as George came to the door. The anal plug was a new experience and the weight and the sensation of being full in that way was distracting her. She wanted more cock. She wanted to feel cock inside of her while her ass was full. And if her pussy was as tight as Mr. V. said, then wouldn't this make it tighter?

She kissed George and accidentally/on purpose knocked him over the arm of Mr. V's couch. She rubbed her body against George until his cock stretched against his pants.

"Do you want to skip the dance?" she asked as she planted her groin over his crotch and rested back on her knees.

She rubbed against his erection for emphasis.

"Sure," he said.

She peeled off her underthings and went for his pants, only pulling them as far as his knees before she swiftly mounted him and plunged his cock into her already used pussy. At first, it was uncomfortable and she wasn't sure if it was that he was bigger than Mr. V or the plug made him feel that way. She didn't care. She rode him hard, took him all and flung herself back, rode him up and down and rubbed her groin into him until her clit screamed.

Mr. V. stood in the kitchen with his coffee in one hand and his now-erect-again cock in the other. Mia moved like a hunting cat, her movements fluid and fast. She didn't stop for anything until her body trembled in hard orgasm.

Mr. V then gave George a warm wet towel, told him to clean up and go home. Once George left, Mr. V took Mia into his bedroom, removed her dress from her, studied her gaping pussy under the lights and then cleaned her with his mouth until she wept from the power of coming again and again. Then they showered and he bathed her and they slept, until it was time for her to go home from the dance.

In Love's Secret Domain

By Dani Brown

Ghosts wandered the Earth dripping ectoplasmic sweat. Thousands of eyes reflect back tin skewers held from skeleton hands. Flies crawled across vacant pupils. Orange orb reflections disguise the emptiness inside.

Honey oozed down the wall. Golden tears landed on dirty sheets. Protect me/protest me. Thin blankets and bed bugs don't keep out the chill.

Ghosts rattled broken chains. Tin miners turned around with a hiss and held their skewers out. Protection. A sense of security only to be proven false. Protest all you want.

No one is around to herd the ghosts. When the ghosts come out everyone disappears. Swallowed by black shadows. Scratching at the seams.

Honey swallowed flies. Never to spit them out.

A tea party waits for the damned at the end of reality. Death's little riddles and mazes tease the damned. First, you have to pass the tests.

Flesh fell from death-kissed cheeks. The voices of long-forgotten angels merged into a long chant. The lighting shifted revealing bodies heaving below forgotten angel feet.

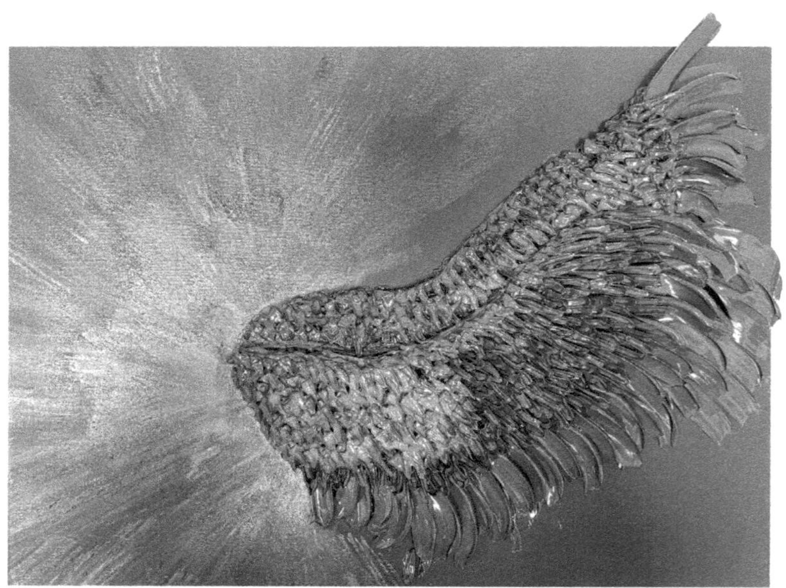

Carnations left by the roadside for a crying lover. A virus lurks within the machine. Flies swallow the image.

Scars criss-crossed angelic arms. Maggots erupted from angelic scars. They never get far in scenes repeated thousands of times. Heaving bodies opened their jaws for a taste of the white falling morsels. The promise of the tea party dimmed.

The bodies heave below forgotten angel feet. Decay slows. But it never stops. Flesh rots in various shades of green. Groaned objections forced angels to flinch. Wing feathers fell into the affray.

Thousands of eyes turned in their sockets and blinked against tin skewers. Honeysuckle blossoms sing in place of unspoken eyeball agony.

Forgotten boys hang from above. Blood washes honey from their thighs. Tin miners feast on flesh, broken into the Void. Orange orbs float above their tattered robes. Their skewers hang discarded from their wrists, until they're needed again. Unlike boys they aren't bred to please.

Erect ghosts drip ectoplasm onto the heaving bodies below. Forgotten angels tried to seal the cracks. And still, the ghosts and tin miners seeped in.

An erection grew inside Sid's pants. The eyes on the walls didn't even pretend to look away. Recording every movement for use at a later date.

Death walked out of the affray. Lips puckered, she went to her knees. How did you get in? Sid didn't have the answers. The tin miners hissed. Lifeless eyes watched from dangling corpses. Honey oozed from Death's lips. Ready for a kiss.

I'm not afraid to die.

The light shifted. Tin miners looked over their cloaked shoulders. Their faces dripped blood and flesh. Flies freed from honey landed on their chins. Light flickered through the cracks. The virus shuddered.

Black tendrils of smoke and decay snaked through heaving bodies. Feathers fell from forgotten angel wings.

Death kissed the tip of Sid's erection with cold lips. Skin left behind perfect lip marks. A new brand of lipstick perfect to market at teenage death girls with a bit of an edge. You shouldn't be here. Her voice massaged the center of Sid's brain.

Forgotten angels flinched. Filtered light burned their skin. Eyes blinked on the walls. They existed in higher concentrations near the cracks. A virus spread through the Void.

A hand wrapped around Sid's ankle. Death's cold fingers traced his collarbone. Flies lazily buzzed. Forgotten angels turned their heads to stare with empty eye sockets.

Fluids leaked out of Death. Vagina to anus soaked through her stolen black jeans. Sid stumbled backwards at the smell, caught by the heaving bodies below. He tried not to breathe. The bodies pulled him backwards towards the cracks. Flies dropped dead on his way past.

Death whispered from the mirror. There is no escape. Sid's cock grew hard. His lover snored in bed. Death spread her thighs. The flesh held together with waxed black threads that swallowed light.

Flies dead along the walls buzzed back to life. Orange patterns lit up along the aged wallpaper. Forgotten angels screeched inside Sid's head. His lover rolled over in bed.

Death held her fingers to the glass. Sid held up his and felt her icy chill kiss his fingertips and travel through his body. Each organ held in a cold embrace.

Feathers fell from Death's decayed wings. The daisy chain on top of her head quivered. Mud tracked across the threadbare carpet. You can't outrun Death.

Cloaked figures stepped out of the wallpaper and formed a shield. Orange lanterns sent flames from their skeleton hands. The flies dropped dead. Sid's lover mumbled in his sleep. My wife mustn't learn of my affair. Sid turned back. You don't have a wife. You never had a wife. His hands rolled into fists of frustration. Death's lust played with his cock.

A jackal barked by Death's boots. Cemetery dirt left footprints through the guesthouse. Mutant cockroaches with white shells swallowed reanimated flies. Ghosts lost ectoplasm through their dicks.

Eyes opened along the aged wallpaper patterns. Sid's lover broke out in a cold sweat. Honey swallowed blood dripping down the walls. Optic nerves weaved together in the hollows and formed organic CCTV.

Death's zippers sang. A recording drowned out the sound. Honeysuckle scraped against the ground floor windows. A cassette tape rewound, lost somewhere in the hollows of the wall.

Ghosts wandered the guesthouse hallways and lingered in door frames. Rats scratched beneath the floorboards. A virus jumped from their fleas.

Death tapped Sid on the shoulder and blocked views of his sleeping lover. Bodies heaved beneath the floor. Flies fell in midflight and died. Cloaked tin miners held orange lanterns high above Sid's lover's sleeping head.

Death caught Sid's lips in her own and sucked on his tongue. Decay spread from the cracks and traced his cheeks.

Ghosts watched in a giant circle jerk that cut through the walls. Rats chewed off mutant cockroach heads and spat them to the threadbare carpet. Dust reacted in a cloud.

Forgotten angels watched Death's dance through cracks in reality. The confidence with which she moved through the scene was nothing more than a mask designed to protect her from the Other.

The jackal bit Sid's ankle. Rats bathed in blood. Heaving bodies tried to regenerate. Cemetery dirt shed from Death's boots buried them again.

Sid's lover sat up in bed. Death stood to the side. Sid's lover's eyes stared into something unseen in the aged wallpaper. His stiff body turned around in the bed. His legs bent at the knees. His bare feet landed on threadbare guesthouse carpet. Sid's lover's eyes reflected orange dancing flames.

Death went to her knees to offer one final release. Sid's lover held a tin skewer out in front. Sid closed his eyes and felt Death's icy chill wrap his heart in a cold embrace at the moment of ejaculation.

Sid's lover dropped the bloodied tin skewer. It bounced on the threadbare carpet. Miners hissed from underneath their hoods.

Only their crimson eyes and orange lanterns could be seen. Black tendrils climbed Sid's lover's legs like wet tentacles. Cockroaches nibbled on his toenails. Flies circled around the guesthouse room.

The Other laughed from the closet. When Death opened it a dead baby with tentacles instead of limbs fell out. Tin miners gathered round and fought over his blue eyes. The cassette tape rewound somewhere in the hollows of the wall.

Blood and fluids dripped on Sid's shoulder. He looked up at boys swinging from their necks. Lifeless eyes dazed and unfocused and completely covered in flies.

The dirty mirror smashed to the guesthouse floor. Ghosts scattered leaving behind steamy puddles of ectoplasmic release.

Heaving bodies grabbed Sid's ankles and pulled him beneath forgotten angel feet. Cockroaches burrowed into the hole left in his heart. Rats pulled out the tin skewer. Eyes watched from the walls, until honey oozed and shut them forever.

The tea party waited at the end of reality. The cakes turned to stone and sat beneath eternal dust. The tea evaporated into the Void.

THEMES: capnolagnia, consensual non-consent, gagging, menage-a-trois, orgasm control, penis play, sado-masochism, switching

Blackhearts

A Kink Noir Story
By William D. Prystauk

My girlfriend's girlfriend.

I hummed the song from Brooklyn's former goth-metal outfit, Type O Negative as I closed my MacBook and glanced over at the woman in question. She sat on the couch reading a German book about healing plants and herbs. I made my way to the bathroom.

My girlfriend Penny's girlfriend is the lovely Vara Black, a Wiccan high priestess, tattooist prodigy from Munich who'd be staying with us for a while.

Might sound strange to many but Penny had no qualms about my boyfriend living with us, so I was relieved to have a chance to return the favor.

Though people had come to call Vara "Ghost Girl" due to her alabaster features and platinum-silver hair, the sinewy vegetarian sported a coil king brown snake on her left leg and a martial eagle backpiece with two full sleeves of animals and flowers in bold color.

The only time I ever saw her cover up her ink was when she portrayed Brian Pulido's hyper-hot and barely clothed in black, Lady Death for Halloween. She went to a party with my beloved Penny decked out as Wednesday Addams, complete with braided pigtails and a container of poison where high-quality scotch laid in wait behind the skull and crossbones.

What the pair did for me that Samhain celebration was cater to my strongest fetish...

Although most people have a fetish, sexual or otherwise, and although most are not considered to be a dangerous or deviant paraphilia, "fetish" continues to endure a negative connotation because we live in an anti-sexual society that's somehow ashamed of body-based fun and exploration. My signature fetish, however, is now almost universally unwelcomed and borders on the lines of taboo because it's no longer acceptable.

Officially, it's called capnolagnia. To everyone else, especially those who have it, those who write about it, and those who sell photographs or make videos about my pleasure, it's a smoking fetish.

I've seen many people at S&M clubs and kink parties who are clearly proud of the desires that drive them, but I'm downright embarrassed. Hell, I think it would be easier to say I have a foot fetish due to its commonality and simplicity. When I asked my therapist if I could get rid of my select fetish, he smiled, held back a laugh, and shook his head "no."

Thankfully, Penny loves her custom-made Marlboro-like, cork-tipped 100s from her tobacconist as much as Vara enjoys her herbal lavender all-white 100s.

And on that Halloween, Wednesday Addams and Lady Death made out like hungry teens and smoked for me. My iPhone almost shutdown because it couldn't hold one more picture or video in its photo gallery of them lighting each other's cigarettes, blowing smoke, inhaling, and looking hotter than ever with cigarettes dangling from their soft lips. All the while, I remained stuck to my underwear thanks to extensive leakage, and my cock begged for release.

The memory enticed me to scroll through the best shots I had saved on my phone and it was difficult to not start jerking off. But Penny would be home soon and as any good boyfriend with a sexually charged girlfriend, I'd save every drop for her.

Most important, she was my Mistress in the bedroom and if I couldn't deliver, there would be Hell to pay and I'd never be able to close out that bill.

Penny texted me. A black heart popped up on my screen.

"Fuck."

This meant she was in the mood to destroy me on a sexual level. Fear and excitement mixed into a torrent and my cock rose to full attention as I washed my hands.

I exited the bathroom to find Vara standing in the kitchen.

She'd often prance around naked but stood before me in white vinyl boots, a short and clinging white vinyl dress, with one of her long white cigarettes dangling from her pink lips. Her granny white hair was in a double Dutch braid or victory roll thing, coming ever so slightly undone at this hour. Vara also had something cupped in her hand I couldn't see.

"Denny," she said in her strong German accent with the cigarette jumping to her words, "you must come with me downstairs."

I didn't hesitate, "Okay."

This was odd because whatever Penny and I did downstairs never included Vara, but my petite Puerto Rican powerhouse had wanted this scenario to happen for some reason.

"Remove your clothes except for your undervear." That was so Penny could unwrap my package in her own sweet time. After I did so, leaving a mess of clothes on the floor, she said, "Open your mouth."

From that cupped hand was the dreaded mouthpiece made especially for me. I took a breath and opened wide and Vara shoved it in. The mouthpiece suppressed my tongue and would keep any screams to a low roar so Penny could continue any torture with a smile instead of having blood spilling from her ears. This meant I wasn't going to be tied up and whipped like some sadomasochistic run-through but torn apart in more severe ways. Vara ripped black tape from a roll, the sound alone made me melt, and she placed the piece firmly over my lips.

"Do not touch your penis," she directed.

* * * * *

Downstairs, in our little dungeon, toys hung from the glowing red right wall, while others sat on shelves, with new additions coming in all the time thanks to Penny's managerial spot at the upper crusty sex store, Pink Sheen. The bondage chair and its stirrups stood at the ready as well as a stool on wheels, and we had a straight-backed red-painted chair of pure cold metal bolted to the floor. The black bondage table rested up against another wall and could easily be pulled anywhere, while brackets in floor and ceiling and their subsequent chains could hold a submissive in an "X" position without the actual Saint Andrew's cross, so Penny could have access to her prize from all sides. There were a couple of ashtrays and two more on stands, and a humidor for Penny's cigarettes as well as the 120 menthols of my boyfriend. We also had enough white, black, and red rope to tie up everyone in this part of Greenwich Village.

Vara took my hand and led me to the red metal chair — the ice-cold red metal chair — and began to tie me down. First, she secured my hands behind the back of the chair so I couldn't change my mind and run away or stop Penny from doing whatever she was going to do. We did CNC anyway, or Consensual Non-Consent. For many practitioners of dominance-submission, that might involve pre-approval of a sexual act that would seem non-consensual and even frightening to others. But I trusted Penny to no end and I never needed to know the plan, especially since she'd cater to some of my likes to keep me engaged.

I was so damn hard as Vara bound my wrists and then my ankles and even the spot above my knees. All the while, she said nothing and her long cigarette hung down firm from her soft lips waiting to be lit — and I wanted her to smoke so bad. But I knew I was in big time trouble when she secured leather straps at the highest point of my legs keeping me locked into the chair. Then she bound my arms together above the elbow. Although that opened my chest a bit wider and allowed me to take in deeper breaths, it was uncomfortable. I knew this meant that this wasn't going to be a "fun pain" episode for me, but a brutal "pain for Penny's pleasure" kind of thing.

"Show Penny how much you love her by not trying to pull avay when she hurts you, understand?"

I nodded. I tried to wiggle but Vara had done an excellent job to keep me secure.

We heard the outside door open and shut. My heart picked up the pace and I began to sweat a little, finally warming up that cold red chair. Vara ran her hand along my thigh and gave me a little half-hug.

"I hope Penny does not hurt you too much for too long," which was the strangest thing to say to a masochistic pain slut like myself. Then again, Vara spent her time healing others, not setting them up to be tortured. I couldn't imagine the conflict going on in her mind, but she loved Penny and wanted to please her, which included her own welcoming of CNC, although I wondered how committed she was to such treatment. I also knew she wanted just a few moments to smoke and take the edge off from the way she accidentally reached for her cigarette and sighed in frustration.

Vara made her way toward the door when Penny entered. Black boots, black stockings, a short leather skirt, a red button-down blouse, and a black lambskin jacket. With her vibrant green cat's eyes lined in black and her blue-black hair in a high ponytail, I was on the verge of collapse. But knowing how best to torture me, she already had that cork-tipped 100 dangling from her red lips.

The woman I loved peered up into the face of Vara. "Where are you going?"

"I… I thought you would like to be alone with Denny."

Penny smiled a little. "I said I had a really bad fucking day and told you to tie him down for me. I didn't tell you to leave the room. And why are you looking at me, you arrogant bitch? Lower your fucking eyes."

Caught off guard, Vara bowed her head and dropped her eyes. "And get that cigarette out of your mouth. You're smoking those 120 menthols you fucking hate."

Vara's face reddened under her eyes. "Yes, my Lady."

My cock got so hard it hurt. I had never seen Penny treat Vara like this but it was play time and they had established this dynamic long ago. I couldn't imagine bearing witness to it.

Vara took the cigarette out of her mouth and brought over the humidor. Standing in front of her Mistress, Vara flipped up the lid. Penny reached in and plucked out a long, all-white 120 menthol. She held the cigarette between her fingers and placed it in the center of Vara's lips. "Keep it in the middle of your mouth. Like a dick."

"Yes, my Lady."

"And since you thought you knew what was happening, you're going to smoke those cigarettes all goddamned night."

The submissive's tone became one of defeat. "Yes, my Lady. Thank you so much."

She told Vara not to light it yet and then ordered her to get the straight-backed chair from the other room.

Penny came over to me. She ran her hands through my long hair. "You look so good all tied up, baby. But I need to gag you better."

She lit her cigarette and shut her eyes as she savored the smoke. After a few seconds, she exhaled a steady stream into my face, which I welcomed. Then she placed the cigarette back into her mouth and retrieved a soft black leather gag from the toy wall.

Penny got behind me, tying the bandana-like gag over the tape and under my mop of hair. "This has to be tight, okay?" I hummed. "Because I have to hurt you a lot so I can feel better. And you want me to have a good time, right?"

I repeated my response though my fear level started to escalate. Penny got in front of me and smiled with the cigarette between her lips as she ran her hand over my hard-on, still trapped under the confines of my black underwear. "Stay hard for me."

Vara brought the chair in as Penny undid the sides to my underwear and slipped off the garment. "Look at all that pre-cum already. You're dripping everywhere." I was glad she was pleased until she said, "Did my bitch get you excited?"

My eyes opened wide and I shook my head like crazy.

Penny didn't care and looked back at Vara. "I need a leather cord and a penis plug. And put a collar around his throat. Chained to the chair."

I groaned as Vara complied.

While she brought the items over in her unsteady hands, Penny took a hard hit of her cigarette. It glowed a bright orange. She exhaled back into my face as she brought the tip of the cigarette to my left nut.

I cried out and twisted my body, or tried to, but there was nowhere to go.

Penny brought a hand to my cheek. "Hey, it's okay." Her raspy voice came on soft and gentle as if she was tucking me in for the night. "You're not being punished. You did nothing wrong. I just had to make sure that bitch tied you down right." Then she turned to her submissive. "See how much his head moved? Get that fucking collar around his neck, right now."

Vara moved quickly. She kept the collar loose.

"What the fuck are you doing? Make it tighter. Think I fucking care if it's hard for him to breathe?"

The sub made the collar cling to my throat like a dress shirt a half-inch too small.

Taking short, hard breaths as I continued to feel the burn on my testicle, I nodded.

Vara returned to her Lady and held out the materials in open palms with her head still bowed and her eyes at the floor. Penny smoked and scrutinized her with disdain while kicking off her attire, save her red blouse.

Taking the items from Vara, Penny blew smoke in her girl's face and said, "Unbutton my blouse." Vara's hands shook. "Look away from me." Vara turned her head and whined. She let her hands feel down the trail of buttons. "You really need to smoke that cigarette, don't you, bitch?"

"Ja, my Lady. Very much."

Penny sat in the chair and laid the cord over her leg. Then she took the three-inch long black plug from Vara, which had a sort of partial silver ring on it, which would lock down under the hood of my cock to prevent it from slipping out. The shaft of the plug was wider and longer than I had been accustomed to. Fear was enough to make me whine and Penny peered right into my eyes.

"Baby, you have been so, so good. But I'm going to abuse the fuck out of you."

Desire and fear mixed once more. My body yearned with an anticipation that kept me breathing hard, sweating, and made my erection painful. Penny had to start soon, whatever in Hell she was planning, because I couldn't take the suspense any longer.

No Surgilube required for insertion because I was dripping like a cheap candle. Penny held the cigarette in her mouth, grabbed my shaft with her left hand, and then shoved the plug into the eye of my erection. I jerked and make noises as she gripped my shaft tighter and drove the plug slowly and deeper into me, which made Penny hum.

"See what happens when you move? That means I have to punish you more."

Vara ran behind me and pressed her hand over my mouth.

"Good girl," Penny said as she locked the plug in place. Then she brought her hand to my cheek again. "Does it hurt?"

I nodded and felt the sweat on my brow. The plug felt like it was spreading my cock wide open from the inside.

"Relax because no matter how bad you need to come or piss, you can't at all. And you can't stop me from doing any-fucking-thing to you."

She smiled as I made noises because my dick wouldn't stop throbbing from the invasion. I had to remind myself that I was blessed because I didn't have a dildo filling up my ass. But that meant Penny wanted me to concentrate solely on whatever pain was coming to my cock.

She blew smoke at me again as she tapped out her cigarette in the standing ashtray.

"Bitch, get by me on your knees." She pointed to a spot to the right of my foot. "Put a cigarette in my mouth and light it. Don't light yours. Because if you do, I'll put it in your mouth backwards."

"Yes, my Lady." Vara's voice was becoming shaky and I heard her struggle with her breathing as well.

"And get that fucking dress off but keep your boots on."

"Yes — "

"Shut the fuck up. Next time to say a fucking word you get a dildo rammed down your throat." Penny stared her down with eyes that burned like lasers. "Remember, you're a goddamned, cheap ass whore and that's it. Three holes to fuck and nothing else." Vara moved so fast, I thought she was going to fall over. "Keep messing up and I'll have Denny fuck your ass. Understand, bitch?"

On the verge of passing out from that idea alone, I watched the cigarette in Vara's ever reddening face begin to shake from her trembling lips. When she put the cigarette in Penny's mouth, Vara could barely work the lighter, which made her Lady groan.

"I need to fucking smoke, so you'd better light my cigarette. Now."

Finally, the flame appeared and Penny tilted her down a little to greet it. She hummed as she inhaled. Vara sniffled.

Penny began to wrap my cock and balls in the leather strap. The cigarette in her mouth moved slightly to her words, "Both of you pussies need to understand this. I want to hurt you because when you cry, I fucking come. And that's the only thing that matters."

I grunted as the black leather separated my balls, squeezing them at the top to make them both round and firm. The leather portion wrapping around the root of my cock made me even harder. Then, Penny pulled at both edges of the cord, strangling my dick.

I roared under the gag.

"Too tight, baby boy?"

I nodded to the point where my neck ached.

"Good. Then I'll make it tighter."

Penny did and I looked down at my ultra-hard dick getting as red as Vara's cheeks by the second. I couldn't relax. Couldn't concentrate. I tried to shift in a sad effort to find comfort that would never happen. And with each breath, I made noises. Little begging noises that got Penny worked up.

"That looks painful," she giggled. "Glad it's happening to you."

Penny stroked me with her left hand and turned to Vara. "You want a light?"

Vara began to speak but shut up and nodded. Penny finally lit the ultra-long menthol for her and Vara drew in a deep inhale as if this was her first cigarette in years. "That's it. Nice and deep. Smoke them like you love them. Right to the filter. Because if you don't love them, then you don't love me."

Vara nodded as she inhaled again, her already narrow cheeks collapsing as she inhaled.

I thought I was going to die. They were both smoking and leaving the cigarettes in their beautiful mouths. My cock was a rock that jumped to my heartbeat. I had to come so damn bad but it was impossible for me.

"Now, burn his dick so I can rub my clit." I grunted already. Vara hesitated for a millisecond because she knew she had no choice. But Penny gave her some incentive anyway. "If you can't do it, I'll tie you up and use your cunt as a fucking ashtray. And you know I fucking mean it."

Vara exhaled and was on the cusp of tears. Penny brought a hand to the back of her sub's neck and rubbed it. "Keep that cigarette in the center of your mouth and put your hands behind your back."

Scared, Vara whined as she complied because she could do nothing else. "You'd better be holding onto your wrist because if your hands come forward, you'll get a beating. Now watch."

Penny inhaled and brought her tip of her cigarette down to Vara's large right nipple. Tears waiting to be released suddenly let go.

"Feel that?"

"Yes… yes, my Lady."

"Nice and warm?"

The submissive nodded.

Penny brought the tip closer to Vara's hard nipple. "Don't you dare fucking move away from me and keep smoking."

Vara mewed as she inhaled, watching the cigarette tip get ever nearer to her skin. Her body began to twist at the hips when Penny suddenly tapped the tip of the cigarette against the nipple. Vara jumped and cried out.

"Did you like that?"

"Ja, my Lady. Thank you for burning me," she sniffled. Then she inhaled again.

"Burn him. I don't care if you keep the tip close to his skin or press it against. But if he's not hurting then you're not doing your job. Grab his dick, pull it, I don't care, but you'd better get him from balls to head. And you get extra fucking points if you don't leave any blisters. Go."

Penny pulled up her legs and slouched in the chair. She held the cigarette in her mouth as the fingers of her right hand began working her glistening pussy.

Vara inhaled and took the menthol from her lips. She kept her eyes on my cock and I heard sharp noises already welling up from my diaphragm. The tip found the base of my cock. A quick strike that made me grunt and made Vara wince. Penny groaned, blew smoke, and handed her cigarette to Vara.

"Burn him with this, too — and don't fucking stop!" Penny cried.

Vara sobbed. She inhaled and ran the hot tips up and down along my shaft as I struggled. She kept the menthol in her mouth while pulling my dick forward to burn its head with the other cigarette. She even kept the cigarette in her mouth as she inhaled and leaned down to burn me. Red marks appeared along my now nearly purple shaft and balls. I kept bucking and crying out and Penny kept groaning and coming.

"Shh…" Penny said when she needed a break to flex her hand. "Be good and take the pain."

Then she told Vara to bring her cigarette to the metal ring so the heat would radiate. "Don't make any noise when she hurts you this time. You can do it, baby. Be strong and just breathe."

The cigarette touched the metal and my flesh. My head rocked back and I took a strained breath. "No noise."

My body twisted and jerked and I struggled to keep the pain inside, but I cried out and Vara pulled the cigarette away though it still felt like it was boring through me.

Penny grabbed her dying cigarette from Vara's hand. She got out of the chair and came at me. I braced myself as she stabbed it out against my right nipple. That was the most I screamed.

"So fucking hot," Penny breathed as she shuttered and came again.

When finished with her menthol, Vara didn't flinch this time. She took her cigarette with its last bit of bright heat and jammed it into my left nipple. The sub twisted it as if it was her ashtray.

Penny fanned her face and got her after orgasm cigarette. Vara lit it for her.

As I fought for air, Penny watched me for a second as she inhaled. She rubbed the back of Vara's neck and then reached between Vara's legs.

"You're lucky you're wet. You must have liked it, you sick bitch."

Vara's cheeks were a brighter crimson and her hands trembled. "Yes, my Lady."

"You are a sick bitch. Very good."

Penny smiled and held her cigarette near Vara's lips. The submissive inhaled deep and hard and the smoke came out of her nose in torrent against the floor.

"Untie his dick before it turns black and falls off."

Penny smoked and watched me pant. Vara released the cord. The unwrapping sent pain throughout my crotch. My balls ached from the tight squeeze and my cock pulsated from the internal agony caused by the penis plug.

With Penny's direction, her sub loosened all my bonds. But my wrists were released only for a moment before being bound behind me again. Vara helped me lay down on the cold floor.

Penny lit a new menthol for Vara. Seeing such a long cigarette in my girlfriend's mouth rocked me. Vara could have jerked me off while I watched Penny smoke, but she put the cigarette between her sub's lips and she immediately inhaled.

"Put your hand hard over his mouth."

Vara did so, half cradling my head between her knees.

Penny flipped up the lock and slowly pulled out the plug. I cried out and sank into the floor when it left me.

My girlfriend laughed a little. "Your dick's going to fucking burn when you shoot your load down my throat."

She lit another cigarette and went down on me, taking my dick full into her mouth. Her tongue glided its way along my shaft. She only stopped blowing me when she wanted to hit her cigarette. Sometimes she'd exhale the smoke over my cock and balls, other times she'd let the smoke leave her nose as she sucked me and hummed.

But in less than two minutes, I felt it and so did Penny. She sped up and I shot cum into her mouth that seemed to burn its way through my dick, causing me to arch my back. Vara kept me down as the searing pain forced me to buck. Penny held on and swallowed and kept on sucking. When I was done and my body rubber, she continued to blow me until she pressed her lips down at the base of my cock and kept them tight as she pulled back as if squeezing the last bit of toothpaste out of a tube.

I was done.

The women rolled me onto my side and released my hands. They rolled me onto my back and they each took a wrist to massage them.

"You okay, baby?" Penny asked.

I nodded.

"Good." She smiled. "You can take the gags off when you're in the bathroom. I know you don't like anyone seeing you like this, but my bitch needs to learn more about what might happen to her."

The massage continued to my arms, neck, shoulders, and they each took a leg. Penny examined my cock and even lifted my balls before the pair helped me get up off the floor.

"You got him everywhere bitch. That's good for you." Then she looked up at me. "And no Band-Aids on your fucked up nipples. I want you to feel how raw they are all week when you put on a T-shirt."

Penny put her arm around me and led me to the bathroom.

Picking up her head, she stood on her toes and gave me a peck on the cheek. "Love you so much. Drink water." Then she shut the door.

I untied the over-the-mouth gag, peeled off the tape, and pulled the mouthpiece out. Man, did I take in a deep gulp of air. I pressed my hands against the sink and leaned down for a while as I came down from my crazy emotional high. Then I downed two glasses of water before stepping into the shower. The spray hurt my ultra-tender nipples as well as my cock and its ceaseless red marks. But I yelled, "Fuckin A!" when I pissed in the shower and realized my urethra was going to burn for a long, goddamn while. I shook from the pain and kept a palm against the wall to hold me up.

When finished drying off, careful to pat my sensitive parts, I tossed the towel aside.

Penny knocked at the door. "Baby? You okay?"

I smiled and opened up. Penny rushed me, putting her hands on either side of my cheeks as she rammed her tongue down my throat. I picked her up. She threw her arms around my shoulders and wrapped her legs around my waist. We continued to kiss as if we'd just been reunited after a rescue.

"Pen, I wish I had the energy to make love to you right now."

She smiled and growled a little. "Well, you can still help me come."

"I can do that. Tongue or fingers or both?"

Penny blushed a little and took me by the hand. In a few seconds, we were back in our playroom.

"How about I play with myself and you burn her tits and pussy for a while?"

Vara, already sobbing, sat bound and gagged in white tape with her legs up in the stirrups. Penny had already shoved some cigarette butts into her ashtray of a pussy. The hapless sub kept on twitching at her crotch.

"Those cigarettes burn, don't they, bitch?" Tobacco's an irritant and Vara was finding out how bad that could be. I hadn't realized how stinging they could be until Penny had used my asshole for the same thing not long ago.

Penny turned to me. "Like I said, I had a really bad fucking day and I've got a long way to go before I feel good."

Vara cried. But when Penny turned from me to get the cigarettes I'd use on her submissive's body, Vara picked up her head and looked at me.

She had that same hungry look in her eyes as I did, and she couldn't wait for us to get started.

Conclusion

So, did you make it through in one piece? Did you plop your peepers down midway, between the mild and the wild and start there or just jump to the last story, or take your time, start at the start and plow, long, hard, and straight through to the end?

However, you played with our juicy bits, we hope you had a good time. The authors here (and I can speak for at least one of them) were hoping to titillate, as much as tickle your imaginations, as maybe spark you to some heretofore unrealized sexual conundrums...as just give you a good read. And, in the end, that's really what Angel and I most wanted. Time is a precious commodity we all seem to have less and less of (or there is just less of it available the older we get) so the last thing Angel and I wanted was to waste yours.

As to what exactly interested, titillated or did anything else to you here, we won't tell anybody, don't worry. And I also have it on good authority, that even if you liked a thing or two you read that you had never heard of (or tried) it might not mean so very much beyond fueling a fantasy or two. Or, it might mean a hell of a lot. That's up to you.

Again, Angel and I won't tell a soul. Your secret needs are safe with us.

One of the authors here, M. Christian and I, are very good friends. We write together, co-host a podcast and have, on occasion, taught at kink conventions across the U.S. And in our experiences at these weekends, Chris (I call him Chris, you call him Sir, got it?!) and I have seen a veritable plethora (and really, the very best plethoras are always the veritable ones) of kinks practiced. My point being, if something you read here indeed prompted a thought, fueled a fantasy or in fact repelled you, just know that somebody else has had that idea, is acting on it now, and it doesn't label you as this or that or anything else.

Thanks for reading *Juicy Bits*. We hope you will look around at all the other Parisian Phoenix Publishing titles and we sincerely thank you for reading this book.

May all your days (and nights) be fun.

Ralph Greco, Jr.

The Fashion and Fiends Series
By Angel Ackerman

Manipulations | Courting Apparitions | Recovery

Angel Ackerman's *Fashion and Fiends* series blends the suspense and fear of contemporary horror fiction with the humor and lightheartedness of late twentieth-century "chick lit." Her diverse network of characters experience the richness and depth of human struggle, which is why while the characters in the universe fall in love and pursue their happily-ever-after, the series can't quite be called paranormal romance.

Ackerman uses magic and the supernatural to explore weighted topics like domestic violence, body image and self-esteem, depression and grief, colonialism, women's rights, coming-of-age, religion, infibulation, infertility, and blended families. As Ackerman's characters navigate their world, they share the same plights their readers do.

Purchase these titles and more at your favorite independent bookseller or online retailer including Bookshop.org.

The saga continues — "Road Trip" — available soon

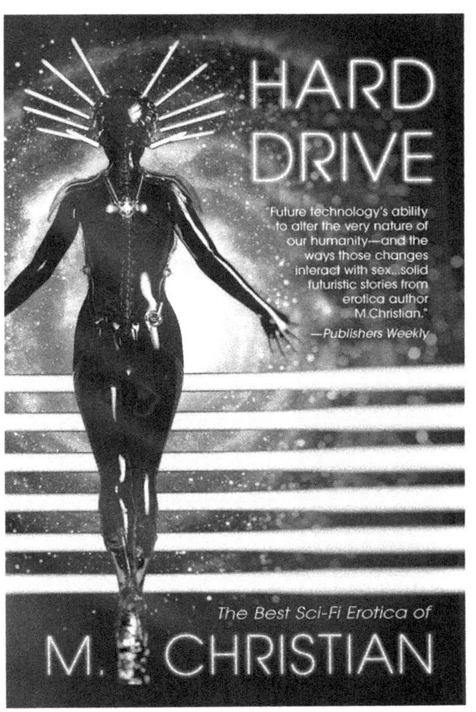

More from M. Christian...

Hard Drive: The Best Sci-Fi Erotica

of M.Christian

Horrorsexual: The Queer Erotic Fright Fiction

Of M.Christian

website: https://zobop.blogspot.com/

More from Ralph Greco, Jr....

Denied: Stories of Male & Female Sexual Ache
DELICIOUSLY NAUGHTY SEXUAL TEASE & DENIAL STORIES

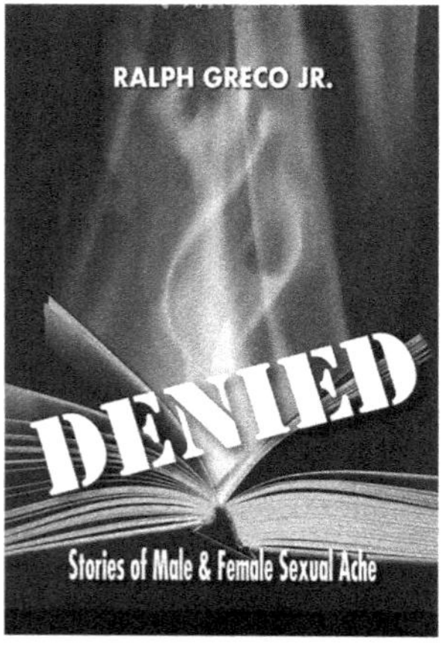

Ralph Greco, Jr. leads the reader through stories of sexual denial where mind games, chastity devices, and relationship dynamics push the characters to their limits both physically and mentally. Whether by friends, neighbors, lovers or strict mistresses, the men and women in Denied will be challenged in the most delicious ways. From lesbian couples dabbling in mutual denial to heterosexual partners embracing new roles, and dirty little secrets being revealed, these stories are sure to have you on the edge of your seat.

 **Buy Now!**

Writing Dirty Words: The non-so-sexy hustle of making a living writing — and the occasional crack of the whip by Darkside contributor, erotica writer, Ralph Greco, Jr.

Ralph's how-to/memoir is the first book from Parisian Phoenix Publishing's newest KINK imprint.

 **Buy Now!**

"

Succumb to Kink Noir

An Award-Winning, Ultra-Hard-Boiled
Erotic Crime Thriller Series

Private investigator, Denny Bowie solves crimes and stops
exploitation in New York City's LGBT and Kink communities
with the help of his girlfriend and boyfriend.

All books available in paperback and for Kindle and Kindle Unlimited.

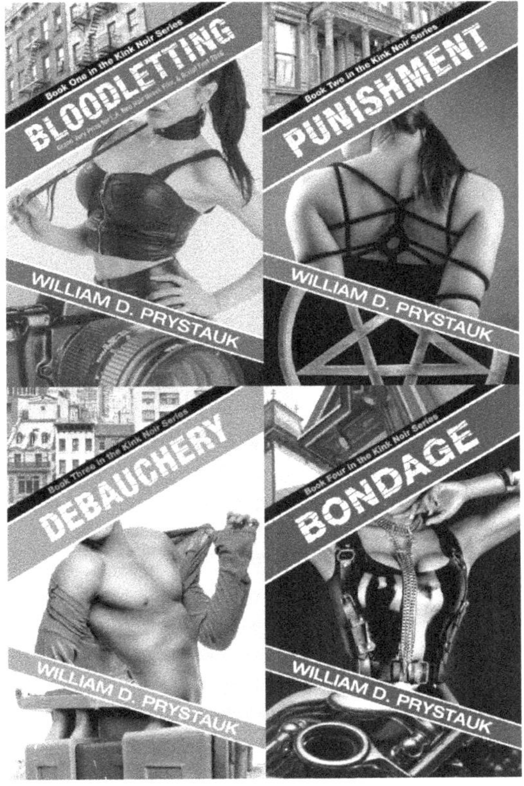

Go to Amazon and type in "Prystauk" to see the novels

Honest reviews welcomed on Amazon, Goodreads, and Bookbub.

"Consent", the fifth novel in the series, arrives in 2024

DO YOU WANT TO HELP PARISIAN PHOENIX OR ANY SMALL PUBLISHER OR INDEPENDENT AUTHOR?

- Buy books. Buy more books. Give books as gifts.
- Recommend authors to friends.
- Share Social Media Posts.
- Leave a review:
  Amazon
  Goodreads
  Google Books
  - Readers use reviews to find books.
  - Retailers' web sites use reviews as part of their algorithm.
  - Some advertisers require a certain number of reviews.
- Join and share newsletters.
- Attend events.
- Join Goodreads and follow authors, mark their books as read, shelve and rate them.
- Check on Patreon and Kickstarter for the creators you love
- Start a book club.

Learn how 

Subscribe to our Newsletter, "Bookish Babble", on

https://parisianphoenixpublishing.substack.com/